THE PRODIGAL CAT

by
Janette Oke

Illustrated by
Brenda Mann

**Other Janette Oke
Children's Books in this Series:**

SPUNKY'S DIARY
NEW KID IN TOWN
DUCKTAILS
THE IMPATIENT TURTLE
A COTE OF MANY COLORS
PRAIRIE DOG TOWN
MAURY HAD A LITTLE LAMB
TROUBLE IN A FUR COAT
THIS LITTLE PIG
PORDY'S PRICKLY PROBLEM

Copyright © 1984
Bethel Publishing Company
All Rights Reserved

Published by
Bethel Publishing Company
1819 South Main Street
Elkhart, Indiana 46516

Cover Illustration by
Brenda Mann

Printed in the United States of America

ISBN 0-934998-19-1

Dedicated with love
to Nancy Roop
as proof that
persistence does pay.

Illustrations dedicated
to my special friend Mary
and her family's two cats
LOIS & CLARK
—BFM

Table of Contents

Chapter 1

The Kittens

The small bit of soft fluff sat on the rug before the patio door, twisting a short stubby neck this way and that. Two sparkling green eyes peered quizzically at the afternoon sky.

The kitten was puzzled. What in the world had happened to the afternoon sun? Even now it should be warming her back as she curled up in its rays. But the sun was not in the sky. The sun was gone. It seemed forever since it had been up there where it should be. Instead, a cold slow drizzle of wet stuff continued to fall. The kitten hated the wet stuff. It clung to her fur and chilled her paws. She objected strongly to going out into it and hid under the sofa or the bed whenever she heard one of the people-persons of the household begin calling. The kitten had learned that, following the calling, the people often came around looking for something or someone. She was never sure who they were calling or for what reason. It seemed that they were always calling someone for something. They were gone now. She had heard the back door close securely behind them as they left the house, so she was safe for the present.

Her eyes continued studying the sky. *Where is the sun?* she wondered. *Is it lost? Can't it find its way up into the sky anymore? Or is it hiding from someone who is calling? Perhaps it is taking a nap and doesn't want to be disturbed.* Then the kitten had a new thought, and she was sure that she had found the answer at last. *I know. It doesn't like the wet either and it doesn't want to come back until it has gone away.*

The kitten felt angry with the wet. What right did it have to chase away the sun? Nobody seemed to like the wet anyway. She had even heard the people-persons complaining about it. Well, there didn't seem to be anything that anyone could do about it. If something *could* have been done, the people-persons would have done it.

The kitten turned her back on the dark day and headed for the bedroom. There was no warmth to be had in front of the patio door. At least the pillows on the bed would give softness and some measure of comfort. The kitten knew that sleeping on the bed had been forbidden, but with the people-persons out she would just take a short catnap.

She curled into a tight ball and tucked her head in among her paws and closed her emerald eyes. It seemed that she had not been sleeping long when she heard the back door again. Quickly she dashed off the bed and sat demurely licking her right paw, as though she had been sitting on that particular spot on the rug all day.

"Here, Mittens. Here, Mittens," a voice soon called from the kitchen. The kitten just cocked her head to one side and waited to see what might happen. She didn't know if the people-person was looking for her or for someone else. If it was for her, did the people-person want to put her out into the cold wet or to give her her dinner? The kitten was hungry and she knew that it wouldn't be wise to hide if dinner was on the way.

"Here, Mittens."

The call was getting close. The kitten listened intently, trying to learn something from the tone of the voice.

"Here, Mittens."

A girl of ten came into the room. The kitten had heard the other people refer to the girl as *Cindy*. The kitten watched the girl curiously. What was she calling about, and who was she searching for this time?

"There you are," cried Cindy. And, before the kitten could even make a dash for the open bedroom door or scoot under a piece of furniture, the girl had scooped her up in her arms.

"When are you ever going to learn to come when you are called?" the girl scolded softly. "You're s'pose to come when you hear me callin' you."

It was too late to run, but the kitten hoped with all of her heart that she wasn't going to be put outside.

Cindy flipped Mittens over on her back and cuddled her close as she headed for the kitchen. Mittens hated this position. She felt so completely helpless lying there with four feet stuck in the air. She longed to flip around and hang onto something solid with her little sharp claws.

"The rest of your family are all eating already," the girl went on. "You'll be lucky if there is any dinner left for you."

The kitten could smell it then—the sharp, distinct odor of cat food that someone always spooned into the common dish just after the strange whirring noise at the kitchen cupboards.

"See," Cindy said. "They are all eating. Tonight you're having chicken."

Cindy was right. There were Mittens' three brothers and one sister busily licking and smacking as they pushed soft, pink noses into the dish on the rubber mat. Suddenly the kitten felt very hungry. She struggled to right herself in

Cindy's arms, but the girl held her firmly until *she* decided to turn her over and drop her gently to the floor.

"Okay, Mittens, if you're not too late," the girl said.

Mittens, thought the kitten. *Mittens—that's me. I must try to remember that, or I'll never get in here in time for my share.*

She shouldered her way to the dish, and her oldest brother pushed her nose aside. A ragged sound rose from his throat. It sounded halfway between a purr and a growl to Mittens. Her brother would need more practice. He growled again, and this one sounded even funnier. Mittens wanted to giggle. A growl from a boy-kitten-turning-cat sounded so funny, but she was too hungry to waste time laughing. Instead she pushed closer, in spite of her brother's warning, and nibbled at the food in the dish.

She didn't like it really—at least not as well as she had liked their mother's warm, sweet milk. But Mother never seemed to be around at mealtime anymore. In fact, they seldom saw her; and when they did she never seemed too anxious to cuddle up with them.

Mittens forced herself to forget about the past and to concentrate instead on getting all that she could from the near-empty dish.

The other kittens left one by one, scattering about the kitchen for one reason or another. Brother Number One snooped along the base of the cupboard, hoping to pick up some tasty crumbs that would serve as dessert. Brother Number Two curled up on the mat by the door and, in no time at all, was having a nap. Brother Number Three began to bat back and forth a small black wheel that had fallen off of one of the small people's toy trucks. The other girl cat sat under a chair and busied herself with licking and washing. She was a most fussy thing and was always primping.

Mittens stayed at the dish, her small tongue busily

cleaning every trace of the chicken dinner from the inside. Round and round the little tongue went, over and over, until not even the tiniest taste of the chicken remained. Still she pushed the dish around, scraping and licking, licking and scraping, hoping that somehow she might find a little more chicken to fill her still-hungry tummy.

Cindy came back.

"You silly thing," she laughed. "It's all gone. Maybe next time you'll hurry. You *must* learn to come when you're called."

Mittens looked up at her with big green eyes pleading.

"Oh, all right. But just this once. Next time you hurry."

Cindy got the can of cat food and spooned a little more into the dish. Mittens dived in nose-first and began to eat hungrily.

I must remember to thank her—later, thought Mittens. She found that she couldn't purr and eat at the same time. She was too busy at the moment, hurrying with the food, lest her brothers and sister return and devour some of her dinner.

The rest of her family did not come. They had all had quite enough. Not one of them even looked toward Mittens as she gulped down her dinner.

By the time Mittens had finished all of the food in the dish, she too had had enough. She licked her chops and her paws, cleaned her whiskers, and then went lazily back to her spot on the rug to see if the sun had come out of hiding.

Still the wet stuff came pattering down, dripping from the rose bushes and making sloppy puddles out under the swing.

Mittens turned away in disgust and headed for her favorite chair. What she needed was a good sleep. She was full now, so she needn't pay any attention if she heard some of the people calling. They would either be calling someone else or would be wanting to put her out. Mittens had no intention of going out into the wet. She wished with all of her heart that it would go away and let the sun come back again. Then she had a terrible thought. Maybe the sun wouldn't be back. Maybe she would never feel its warm rays on her fur again. Maybe the sun had deserted them for good.

Chapter 2

That's Enough!

When Mittens crawled into the kitten box that night and curled up with her brothers and sister, the rain was still falling steadily and a chill wind blew. Mittens could not see out, because the curtains had been pulled across the windows. She could hear the wind blowing and thought that it sounded like some old, old people-person moaning and groaning. She pressed her body close against her sister and Brother Number Two and tried to shut out the sound with the soft noise of their breathing.

The older people were still busy about the house, and the funny box with flashing pictures and many sounds was flickering in the corner of the room. Sometimes Mittens found the mysterious box fascinating, but she didn't like it now. She wanted to sleep. She wanted to forget that the sun had left them. She wished that she knew where it had gone. She would like to go after it and coax it to come back to them. Maybe if the wet would go away, the sun might eventually come back again. Mittens was thoroughly disgusted with the wet.

At last she was able to sleep. The noisy, flashing box was

turned off, and the older people-persons went to their soft bed. All of the lights were sent away, just as the sun had been sent from the sky. Mittens curled up more tightly and slept until morning came.

Her first thought of the morning was of the dreaded wet. She was always put outside the very first thing in the morning and she hated the thought. Maybe if she jumped up quickly and ran for a bedroom, she could be safely hidden in a corner under a bed before the girl Cindy or one of the other people came looking for her. She was about to bound out of the bed-box, when a pair of hands reached down and scooped her up.

"Time to go out," said Cindy. And, though Mittens tried to wriggle free from her hands, she was carried to the door and shoved outside. She stood still, pushing her body as close to the big door as she was able. If she stayed closely pressed to the house, the wet might not reach her. Then she looked out at the back yard and began to realize that the wet had stopped falling. There were still many puddles about the yard and the trees and shrubbery still dripped large droplets of water, but the wet was no longer coming from the sky. Mittens looked for the sun, but it was not there. It was just as she had feared. The sun had gone away. Heavy dark skies were all that she could see where the sun should be.

Mittens left the comfort of the back step and worked her way slowly across the lawn. She stopped every few steps to lift a chilled paw and shake the wetness from it. She was not long in returning to the steps, where she joined her brothers and sister who were also crying to be let in. Cindy soon came, and all five cats bounded into the kitchen and began, in unison, to coax for their breakfast.

After eating her fill and washing her face and paws, Mittens turned her thoughts to other things. She felt like

playing but could see nothing nearby to play with. Brother Number One sat up on a chair nearby, his long tail hanging down over the edge and swishing back and forth as he watched the boy-person's goldfish swimming back and forth in its bowl. Mittens watched for awhile, her eyes traveling back and forth, back and forth, with each swish of his tail.

Suddenly she pounced and caught the tail firmly in her sharp kitten teeth. Brother Number One let out a howl and sprang from the chair, but Mittens had not released his tail yet. He was jerked to a stop mid-air, and Mittens was pulled forward by the motion. Brother Number One let out another shriek and turned toward Mittens, his anger showing in his standing fur and sparking eyes. By then, Mittens had realized just what she had done and what might be the results of her actions. She released the tail and, tucking her own tail against her body, streaked for the bedroom and the safety of the dark corners under the bed. Brother Number One was not to be so easily evaded and he followed closely on her heels, swatting her now and then with an angry paw.

Mittens dashed under the bed, but Brother Number One followed. Mittens ran for the closet. The door was closed. She made a dash for the sofa, with Brother Number One growling and threatening close on her heels. Under the sofa Mittens ran, but Brother Number One was still close behind her. On ran Mittens, back across the family room and into another bedroom. Brother Number One had still not given up the chase.

Mittens heard a loud crash as something came tumbling to the floor, flying into many pieces as she dashed by. She slowed just enough to squeeze her slim body under the dresser. Brother Number One tried to follow, but his head was too large to give him entrance. He clawed and growled and spoke angry words at Mittens, who lay scrunched down beneath the furniture, her head bumping the board above her and her chin scraping the floor beneath. It was not a comfortable place to be, but at least for the time she was safe.

She held her breath in silence, hoping that Brother Number One would soon go away. At last he did, but Mittens was still afraid to come out. Her body ached for a chance to stretch itself. Her head wanted to be lifted up, but there was no way that she could lift it. Even her tail seemed to cramp from the position that she was forced to maintain. Brother Number One had gone away, but would he still be lurking out there, waiting for her to appear? Mittens dared not chance it; and so the day gradually wore on as she crouched, cramped and stiff, beneath the dresser.

Now and then she heard the clock in the hallway strike. She heard the birds chirping and quarreling outside the bedroom window. She heard the kittens playing as they raced back and forth in a game of tag or had a wrestling match to see which was the stronger. She heard the occasional fight as one kitten was a little rougher in his play than the other one wished him to be. At length she heard the back door open and close, and people voices began to fill the house. Still she crouched where she was. She began to be fearful that, when it was time to come out, she might no longer be able to make her legs work again. What if she would have to stay cramped and crowded beneath the dresser forever? Would she really be able to move again?

And then Mittens heard a loud voice, and the people-person of the house was exclaiming angrily about whatever had gone crashing to the floor.

"It's those kittens," she said in almost a shout. "If we don't get them out of here soon, we won't have a decent thing left in the house. Look! Just look at this lamp! That's the second one this week. I won't put up with it a moment longer. I want them gone. All of them. Tonight."

Cindy's voice was the next one to be heard. There were some more people talking in the kitchen. Cindy pleaded, but the older people-person kept saying, "No, they've all got to go. You have Tabby—that's enough. I want all of them taken to the animal shelter. Tonight. They'll find them all good homes."

Mittens could hear Cindy calling. She called one name after another, and finally Mittens heard the call, "Here, Mittens. Here, Mittens."

Mittens knew that she must creep out from under the dresser, but she was still fearful. What would Brother Number One do when she made an appearance?

Slowly she tried to pull herself forward, but she soon found that she couldn't move. Terror struck her heart. It was true. She would never be able to move again. Maybe that was what had happened to the sun. Maybe someone had driven him into a tight place and he was no longer able to get himself out. Mittens tried harder, but there was just no room for her body to move.

Again and again Cindy called. "Mittens, come here. You're going to miss your dinner again."

Mittens tried to be calm. *Think,* she told herself. *You got in here. You must be able to get out.*

I came in from that way, Mittens reminded herself. *Maybe I can go back out that way.* But Mittens was not able to turn around.

Maybe I can back out. Mittens tried and found that she could move a very short distance. Little by little, a fraction of an inch at a time, Mittens backed slowly and painfully out from under the dresser. At last there was only her head remaining, and with an eager pull Mittens attempted to pull herself free. She forgot that she needed to twist her head slightly to get it to come out, and the dresser caught her on the top of her head and shoved her chin cruelly into the floor. With a sharp little cry, Mittens stopped short and tried again, this time taking the time to do it properly.

At last she was free. She moved slowly across the room. She wanted to run to the kitchen, but her legs were too stiff. Her head hurt and her jaw ached from the jarring that it had received. She knew that she would be late for dinner again, and she was so hungry.

As she moved slowly into the kitchen, Cindy bent to scoop her up into her arms. Everything hurt. Mittens closed her eyes against the pain. How could Cindy know that she ached all over?

"You're late again," Cindy said. But instead of scolding her, she stroked her softly.

"All the food is gone, but I'll give you some more. There's no use saving it anyway if I won't have any kittens to feed it to."

She put Mittens down on the kitchen floor. Mittens felt a thankfulness that Cindy hadn't dropped her to the floor. Even a few inches would have jarred her stiff legs and body.

Cindy got out the can of food and spooned some into the dish, and Mittens began to eat. Even eating hurt. The bruised jaws didn't want to work right; and if Mittens had not been so hungry, she would have turned and left the dish of cat food setting there on the blue rubber mat.

She chewed slowly, trying to favor the injured jaws. When she had had enough to quiet her growling stomach, she walked slowly away from the dish and began to groom herself, hoping that somehow in doing so some of the pain might be washed away also.

She still hadn't seen Brother Number One. She could hear the other kittens playing in Cindy's bedrom. They were running back and forth and climbing up and over the bed and then to the window and down across the bed table. At last there was another big crash, and Cindy cried out and ran for her room. The big people-person cried out too, but her voice was much louder and angrier than Cindy's.

"See what I told you," she said. "We have to get them out of here. All of them. They are going to wreck everything in the house."

"It's only a bottle of cologne," defended Cindy. "And I didn't like it anyway. It didn't even have a nice smell."

"Nice smell or not, you are going to be smelling it for a long time. We'll never get that out of your carpet."

"That's okay," Cindy changed her mind. "It smells kinda good."

The big people-person laughed in spite of herself.

"Oh, Cindy," she said, more softly now. "I know that you hate to give the kittens up, but we have to. You can understand that, can't you?"

Cindy was quiet for a moment. At last she answered in a shaky voice. "I know. I just didn't want to give them away so soon, and I wanted to find them homes myself."

"But that didn't work." The big person was talking more quietly now. "You tried—but no one seemed to want kittens. The shelter will find good homes for them. Promise."

"Is Daddy gonna take me?" asked Cindy.

"No, I'll take you. Just as soon as you are ready."

The smell from the broken cologne bottle had even reached Mittens in the kitchen. Her nose began to twitch and she felt like sneezing. She wondered if her brothers and sister had disappeared after the crash. She supposed that they were hiding somewhere in the deepest and darkest corners under the bedroom furniture.

Cindy began to seek them out. One by one she found them and deposited them into a meshed carrying box. When she had rousted all three brothers and one sister from the confines of bedroom hiding places, she came back to the kitchen to look for Mittens.

"There you are. Still right here where I left you. You weren't chasing around being bad. You're always good. I should be able to keep *you* anyway."

Mittens was glad that she would not need to confess about the lamp and what had happened to it earlier in the day.

Cindy opened the door of the carrier and placed Mittens gently inside—right up tight against big Brother Number One. Mittens held her breath, wondering just what her brother might do to get even. He nosed her gently and welcomed her in, and Mittens released her breath again. He held no grudge about the earlier events of the day and had already forgiven and forgotten. Mittens eased her aching body down onto the soft mat on the floor of the carrier and began to lick her aching muscles.

Chapter 3

Moving

It occurred to Mittens that the crowded and funny box was a strange place to be bedded for the night. They had always slept together in their roomy large cat-bed in the family room. Now they had all been shoved into this small, drafty thing with the smell of other cats still lingering on the mat at the bottom. It seemed to bother Brother Number Three and he mewed and fussed to be let out. Sister tried to shush him but he cried all the more. Mittens was still too sore and aching to have concern for the new bed that they had been given, even though it wasn't to her liking. Brother Number Two, who never allowed anything to bother him, curled up in a tight ball and fell asleep. Brother Number One complained that the sleeping cat was taking more than his fair share of room, but that didn't bother Brother Number Two any—he still slept on. Brother Number Three was pacing back and forth trying to find a way out. He kept walking all over the rest of them, and all but the sleeping Brother Number Two began to complain about it.

"I wish you'd lie down an' keep quiet," said Brother

Number One irritably.

"I have no intention of sleepin' in a place like this," Brother Number Three growled in return.

"I don't see that you have much choice."

"There's gotta be a way out of here," insisted Brother Number Three, and he continued to climb all over the rest of them. Brother Number Two went right on sleeping.

Cindy was soon back. She spoke to the kittens through the wire over the end of the box and tried to calm Brother Number Three, but even that didn't help. Then she picked up the carrier and left the house, her mother walking along behind her, rattling keys in her hand.

Suddenly Mittens realized where they were going. The kittens had never been in the shiny big blue thing that the family was always going off in. Many times they had watched from the window as the thing gobbled up the whole family and went charging down the street. It never seemed to hurt them and always returned later to spit them all out again. Mittens was rather excited about the adventure now as Cindy pushed the carrier box into the insides of the big blue thing. Mittens had always been the most curious one of the litter, and she did want to see just what happened when one was swallowed up by the big blue monster that always brought you back home again.

There was a strange noise and then motion. Sister looked wild-eyed and jumped right across sleeping Brother Number Two and right into pacing Brother Number Three. It didn't do her any good. She was still in the funny box, going off somewhere with all the rest of them.

They soon got used to the motion. Even Sister settled down and the terror left her eyes. Mittens wished with all of her heart that she could see something and pushed her way to the wire end of the box. She pressed her nose against the hard mesh and tried to twist so that she could see what was happening. It wasn't any use. All that she could see was the inside of the thing that had swallowed them.

After riding for awhile, the motion stopped and the noise stopped too.

We're home again, thought Mittens. She would be glad to get out of the cramped quarters. She was tired of being tramped on by her brother.

There was slamming and banging as Cindy and her people-person mother got out of the big blue thing; then Cindy was lifting the box out. Mittens could see now. They weren't back home at all. They were at a place that Mittens had never seen before.

Cindy carried them—swinging back and forth—on down the walk and through the big door. She placed them on the floor and followed her mother across the room to where more big people-persons were sitting at desks. They talked for a while, their voices soft and empty-sounding; then the box was being lifted again and carried through another door.

When Cindy reached into the box to lift the kittens out, Brother Number Three made a leap for it. He scratched Cindy's arm in the process and made her squeal in pain and anger. He fled past all of the big people-persons and down a long row of funny cages. Dogs began to yell at him, all in unison, from what seemed like hundreds of directions at once. Brother Number Three skidded to a stop and looked around, his eyes big and frightened. He seemed to be wondering if he should return to the safety of the carrier box or keep on running.

One of the big people-persons ran after him. Brother Number Three saw him coming and made another dash for safety. But there was no place to go. He soon was in a corner, the sound of the barking dogs all around him and the big people-person right behind him. Cindy's mother went to help the other person, and it wasn't long until

Brother Number Three was held tightly in the arms of the man in the long green coat.

It was after all of the commotion had subsided that Mittens began to notice the smell. She didn't like it. The whole place was a riot of smells of many different animals. There were other smells too—strong mediciny smells and sharp pungent smells of left-over animal food. Mittens wished to be away from the whole disagreeable place and hoped that Cindy would hurry up so that the blue monster could gobble them up and take them home again.

Instead of heading back out the door, they were all taken from the carrier box and placed in a larger—but still uncomfortable—wire pen. They could see out now, at least in one direction. There were many such pens in the room. A number of them housed other cats. There were many others that contained those horrible barking dogs, their enemies of the neighborhood. Mother had warned them never to tangle with a dog but to head for the nearest tree or post. Mittens looked for a tree or post now but could not see one. All of the kittens were nervous. They didn't know but what at any moment one of those barking dogs might throw himself at the wire mesh and come charging right through it at them. Even calm Brother Number Two looked like he might never dare to go to sleep again.

Mittens did wish that they could hurry and get out of there. It seemed like a terrible place to be. Cindy reached a hand through the little flap up over the door and tried to stroke each one of them one last time. Their bodies arched as they all backed away, hisses escaping from their kitten mouths.

"They'll soon settle down," said the man in the funny green coat. "They feel a bit upset right now with everything strange, but they'll be all right."

Cindy looked a bit doubtful. But, at the urging of her mother, she picked up the carrier box; and then the two of them followed the green-coated man out the door, and the door closed with a swish behind them.

Mittens thought it very strange that Cindy had forgotten to put them back in the tight-fitting carrier box. Maybe they had complained too much and Cindy thought that they didn't want to ride in the box any more. For a moment Mittens felt angry with Brother Number Three. He was the one who had done so much fussing. Now see where he had gotten them!

Mittens looked around at the other members of her family. Brother Number Three was still pacing back and forth, though Mittens noticed that he stayed as far away from the front of the enclosure as he could. He wanted no encounters with those dogs. Brother Number One was peering this way and that, trying to see if he might find some way out of the mess. Sister still looked frightened and cowered in a corner, not even interested in her grooming. Her hair was mussed and there was dirt on her nose, and she didn't even seem to care. Brother Number Two was the only one of them who seemed to be his typical self. He yawned, curled up in a ball, and tried to get some sleep in spite of the noise and commotion all about him.

For once Mittens agreed wholeheartedly with Brother Number Three. She didn't like this place either. She didn't like the smell, she didn't like the noise, and she most certainly didn't like sharing quarters with all of those hateful dog-creatures. She made up her mind that she was going to get out—and the sooner the better. She joined Brother Number Three in his pacing. Back and forth, back and forth they went, pressing their noses into the corners, pushing their shoulders against the wire, scratching and clawing; but nothing would give. At length, exhausted, she fell down beside her sister. Already all of the other members of the family were sleeping. Even Brother Number three had given up and joined them. Mittens decided that she would sleep too—but only for awhile. Then she would find a way out.

Chapter 4

Temporary Quarters

The noise wakened Mittens. She had never heard such a commotion. It seemed that every dog in the world must be caged up in that one small room, trying desperately to out-bark one another. The cats mewed too, but one could not even hear them over the din that the dogs were making. Mittens would not have even known that they were speaking, if she had not seen the movement of their mouths as they paced back and forth at the front part of their cages.

It was soon apparent what had caused all of the clamor, for two green-coated people were moving down the long line of cages filling dinner dishes and sloshing water into jars. Mittens was reminded of how thirsty she was and looked about for a water dish like the one that they had back home on the blue rubber mat. There was none. All that their cage seemed to have was a funny-looking con-traption hooked to the side of the cage. Even as Mittens looked, Brother Number Two uncurled himself, yawned and stretched—quite oblivious to the noise, the smell, and the surroundings—and then moved lazily to the funny con-traption on the wall and began to lick at it and smack his lips. It was water. Mittens had never seen water offered in such a fashion before. She rushed over to Brother Number Two and tried to push her way in for a drink as well, but only one could drink at a time. Brother Number Three arrived just as she did and he was bigger than Mittens, so his turn came first. Then it was Brother Number One shoving her aside. Mittens thought that surely she would perish before she could ever get a drink, and slapped hard at Brother Number One's nose. He slapped back and the fight began. They wrestled and shoved and bit at one another. While they fought, Sister calmly moved in and helped herself to the water. Then Brother Number Two, who had been shoved aside by all of them, took another turn.

The fight ended with Mittens the loser. She fled to a far corner of the wire room and licked her wounds, and Brother Number One made a face at her and shouldered his way to the water jar. He took his time at it too. Mittens had never seen anyone drink so much or take so long doing it. At last he moved aside, still licking and smacking his lips. Mittens moved cautiously to the jar for her turn, but it was empty. Every bit of the water was gone. She wanted to sit down and cry.

The green-coated people were getting closer and closer. The smell of food was stronger and the scent of the fresh water nearly drove Mittens crazy. Less dogs were barking now, for most of them were far too busy gulping down food to have time to make such a fuss.

At last one of the people-persons reached the kittens' cage. He unhooked a little door and reached in for the water jar. Mittens wanted to swat at the stealing hand. If it took the jar, how would she ever get a drink? She knew that it was empty now but it might get some water if it was left alone. If the green-smocked people-person took it, there was no hope at all. Mittens might have fought for the

jar if she had not already been smarting from the bite of Brother Number Three. Instead she backed into a corner and wept.

The big hand was soon reaching into the cage again and this time, to Mittens' amazement, it was replacing the water jar. Mittens knew from the smell that the water jar was no longer empty. She could smell the fresh water all across the cage. She ran for it, forgetting even to be fearful of the hand that had not been withdrawn.

Then the hand was gone for a moment, and Mittens licked thirstily at the droplets of water. How good they felt on her dry throat.

The hand reached in again, and this time a dish of food was placed on the wire floor of the cage. All of the kittens rushed for it. Mittens was still too busy drinking to hurry for the food. The other kittens gulped down the food quickly; and by the time that Mittens had finished her drink and went to join them at the food dish, the meal was almost gone. Mittens ended up on the short end again, and this time there was no Cindy to coax for more. Mittens moved to the front of the cage and meowed to call the people-persons. They had moved far down the aisle of cages and were much too involved in what they were doing to pay any attention to one small kitten. Mittens doubted if they could have heard her anyway. The noise of unfed dogs and cats was still too great. She gave up and turned back to lick again at an empty dish.

Sister was washing now. She seemed to once again be concerned with the condition of her shining coat. Brother Number Two had gone back to sleep, and Brothers Number One and Three were having a play-wrestle in the middle of the cage. They kept bumping into Mittens and the empty dish as they rolled and snarled and rocked back and forth.

The game looked fun, and when Mittens had decided

that it was useless to lick at the dish anymore she decided to join them. Even Sister became involved. For several moments they tussled and rolled and bit playfully at one another. The game ended when Sister's sharp teeth came down too tightly on Brother Number Three's tail. With a shriek and a sharp smack of his paw, he sent Sister reeling backwards. She cried out that he was a big bully, but the game was over. Sister went to a corner of the cage to put her coat back in order, and Mittens took another corner and decided to be very still for a few moments until Brother's anger subsided.

The noise outside began again. It was not as bad as before the meal, but dogs were barking again. It seemed that they had nothing better to do; Mittens supposed that dogs just always barked. That seemed to be about the only thing that they knew how to do.

Mittens began to get sleepy and decided to join Brother Number Two in the corner. She curled up with him and had not even dropped off to sleep before Brother Number One crawled in beside her; and then it was Sister, curling close and bringing warmth to her other side. Mittens snuggled down between them and closed her eyes. She tried to ignore the barking of the dogs and the fussing of the other cats. She still hated the smell. She still didn't like the feel of the wire mesh beneath her. She still wanted to be out, but she could wait. She would have a nap first and then work on the problem. What more could possibly go wrong? First the sun had gone away because of all the wet. Then they had been bundled up and brought to this strange and noisy place in the big blue monster. Then Cindy had walked away with the carrier box, forgetting to put them back in it. Then she had missed her fair share of the dinner because she had been too thirsty to leave the water jar. Now her little tummy complained because it was not full enough to be content. *Well, surely on the morrow,* Mittens thought, *I'll be able to sort it all out. Maybe if we all worked together we could find our way home again.*

Chapter 5

Boredom

Morning came. It wasn't sunlight that told the kittens that another day had begun, for there were no windows to show them the outside sky. It was the noise of their fellow-prisoners and also the gnawing of their own stomachs that woke them. It must be time to be fed again.

Brother Number Three was the first one to crawl from the warm circle of kitten bodies and stretch and yawn to meet the new day. Sister followed. She did not even stretch but went right to grooming her silky coat. Brother Number Two complained some at being disturbed and then curled up by himself and went back to sleep again.

Mittens decided that she had had enough sleep for one night. It occurred to her that it was the right time for them to be searching for a way out of this place. Then Mittens remembered Cindy and the strange carrier box. By now Cindy would have discovered that she had forgotten the kittens, leaving them behind. She would come back for them in the big blue noisy machine as soon as she could. There was no need for the kittens to try to find their way home. All that they had to do was to wait for Cindy.

Mittens yawned and smiled to herself and went to curl up with Brother Number Two. She couldn't sleep; it was far too noisy in the place. Every dog seemed to be trying to outbark his next door neighbor. The cats could even be heard occasionally, though their voices weren't nearly as loud as the dogs'. Mittens wondered how Brother Number Two ever managed to sleep through it all. She tried again, shutting her eyes tightly, but that didn't help one bit to keep all of the sound from vibrating round and round in her head. Then Sister and Brother Number One began a game of tag, and it sounded like so much fun that Mittens couldn't resist opening one eye to see what was going on. Sister was chasing Brother over the feeding dish and around the corner, leaping over sleeping Brother Number Two and on around past the food dish again. The game reversed and Brother was now chasing Sister. In turn, they leaped upon the drinking jar and down to the wire floor again in one swift motion, still running as their feet hit the floor. Back they came again, sailing across Mittens as they ran. Mittens ducked her head and closed her eyes, thinking that surely one of the flying feet would kick her as they passed over. Somehow they managed to clear her, but by now the game had challenged Mittens as well. She bounded up from her place on the wire flooring and chased after them, wild with the excitement of the game.

They ran back and forth, back and forth, up and over, under and around, until Mittens felt that her feet were flying. She expected Brother Number three to join in the fun but he was busy scratching at the wire enclosure, trying to find a way out. Mittens could not hear what he was grumbling about, but she was sure that he was still unhappy with where they had been shut up and was determined that he wouldn't spend another night in the place.

Cindy will soon be here. She'll get us out, Mittens wanted to assure him; but she didn't have the breath to call out to him as she dashed about the cage.

At last all three of the kittens collapsed in an exhausted heap on the floor of the cage, their sides still heaving from the exertion. It was time for another short nap. Still wearing happy expressions, they fell into a deep sleep again. Brother Number Two had not even stirred, and Brother Number Three still paced and scratched, paced and scratched.

When Mittens awoke again, it was to even wilder and more excited barking. The green-smocked people-persons were passing down the rows of cages again, filling food dishes and replenishing water jars. Mittens realized at once just how hungry she was and was not late getting to her breakfast. She ate as quickly and as much as any of her family members.

After breakfast they were too full to play for awhile so they washed themselves carefully and then scattered about the cage to entertain themselves in various ways. Sister continued her grooming. Mittens watched her for a few moments, marvelling at the way that Sister would wash, over and over again, the already spotless coat. Then Mittens lost interest in Sister's grooming, and moved to the front of the cage, looking out at what was before her.

Two large cats occupied the cages across from them. They did not share the cage but each had one of his own. They didn't seem to be on very friendly terms. They weren't saying anything, but Mittens could see the hostility in their eyes. The big black tom paced back and forth, back and forth, sending warnings to the other cat with the arch of his back and the fire in his eyes. The orange cat, another big tom, returned the stare with cold, green eyes, his whiskers twitching now and then and his tail giving an occasional flick. He did not pace; only his eyes followed the movement of his neighbor.

In the next cage was a tiny pup. He was of mixed breed

and seemed to be having the time of his life all alone. He rolled and tumbled and chased his tail. He somersaulted and high-jumped and twisted and turned. He was clumsy but he surely looked to be having fun.

In the next cage was a half-grown dog. He had black spots on white, or white spots on black—Mittens wasn't sure which. He looked bored as he lay with his head on his paws, his eyes dark and listless. Mittens let her eyes pass over him quickly and go on to the next cage. It held a big dog with long shaggy hair. He stood with feet firmly planted, barking and barking, though Mittens couldn't see one thing for him to be barking at. In the next cage was a mother dog and three nursing puppies. Mittens couldn't get a good look at them, for the mother was lying toward the back of the cage and they were too far away for Mittens to see well.

Mittens could not see who occupied the cages on either side of the one that the kittens inhabited. She knew that they had neighbors. She could smell them there. On the right side it would seem that there were other cats, and on the left there were dogs of some kind.

Mittens turned her eyes in the other direction and followed that line of cages. Beside the two angry cats was a big, black dog. She looked old and a little stiff. She never seemed to be angry or upset. She did not bark noisily. The only response to any outside activity was an eager pressing of her nose against the wire wall and a wagging of her tail.

In the cage next to her was a young dog, though already he was big. His paws seemed to flatten all over the wire floor and his floppy ears looked about to pull down his head. Mittens wondered how he ever kept the ears out of his food dish when he ate. She would watch him sometime just to see.

In the next cage was another cat. She was beyond the kitten stage and was thin and rather shabby. Mittens

wondered about her. She didn't seem too active, and as Mittens watched her for many moments she didn't see her move—not even once. Mittens passed on to the next cage.

In that cage, too, was a cat. He was even bigger than either the orange or the black tom. He looked mean. Mittens felt relief pass through her that there were two sections of wire mesh separating them. She was quite sure that this tom wouldn't take kindly to rambunctious kittens. In fact, she didn't expect *that* tom to take kindly to anyone. He had a scar across his forehead and one ear lay ragged and floppy. Tufts of hair seemed to be missing here and there, and his tail had an odd crook in it.

As he sat and stared out of his cage, Mittens got the impression that he was very much aware of everything that went on. She was sure that *he* knew, too, who lived in each of the cages. His eyes were yellow slits in his big, battered face; they moved back and forth, carefully noting all that went on before him. His tail lashed angrily back and forth, looking comical because of the crook in it. Mittens wanted to laugh at the funny sight: the tail flopped forward, then flopped back, twisting in a strange way with each sweep across the cage floor. It looked like something that would be tremendously fun to chase. Mittens could imagine herself pouncing upon it and sinking her sharp little teeth into it to try to keep it from shuddering across the wire floor again.

Mittens checked herself and backed up a few paces, lest the big cat in the wire enclosure be able to read her mind. She had no intention of having all of that caged-up anger turned in her direction.

Sister came up beside her.

"What are you lookin' at?" she asked.

Mittens' eyes did not leave the big cat.

"Look at him," she whispered.

Sister looked directly across at the two across-the-hall

toms.

"No, not them. The big one, down there."

Sister followed Mittens' eyes and spotted the big cat. She backed away one pace and then stood, her eyes transfixed, staring at the cat as his tail thumped back and forth angrily on the floor of his cage. Mittens turned her eyes from the cat for a moment so that she could see the reaction of her sister. Sister just stared, her body rigid and her eyes big.

"He's big, isn't he?" whispered Mittens, as though she feared that the big cat might hear her.

Sister nodded her head but her eyes did not leave the big cat.

"He looks mad," she finally said in a scared voice.

"Don't worry. He can't come in here."

At that moment the large cat turned his eyes directly on them. His cold stare fastened on them, seeming to pin them to their spots on the wire cage floor. Mittens felt that she was unable to move. The yellow eyes seemed to go right through her, making her frightened and defenseless. Sister must have felt it too for Mittens could sense her body shrink, though she did not move a muscle. The cat sat, his eyes staring, his tail still lashing with its foolish flip-flop motion. Then, with contempt, his eyes slid over them and passed on to the cage beside them.

Slowly Sister began to back away into the depth of the cage. Mittens aroused herself and moved with her. They said nothing, but it was good to bump into the sleeping form of Brother Number Two. Mittens let herself fall down beside him and snuggle up to his warmth. She felt cold all of the sudden, though she was quite sure that the temperature in the cage had not changed. Sister, too, snuggled in with them. Brother Number Two stirred somewhat but did not object to them joining him. Mittens curled even closer to him and tried to sleep. At first all that she could see were those big yellow eyes, staring, staring, at her. She tried to block them out of her mind. They were there. She shut her eyes more tightly. They still followed her. She turned over. They were still there. She turned her thoughts to Cindy—Cindy and the carrier box that would be coming soon to take them all to the people-person home again. At last she was able to shut the image of the big cat out of her mind, and sleep came.

She slept soundly for awhile and then she was dreaming.

The wire front to all of the cages had been stripped away. All of the animals were free to go and come as they pleased. The big, black dog with the stiff legs still stood in her cage, her tail still waving signs of friendship. She did not bark or clamor for attention, but smiled faintly as though she was truly happy that the wire mesh was no longer pressing against her nose. The puppy did not leave his cage either. He was much too busy tumbling around and chasing his tail. The black and the orange toms faced each other for the first time, having eyes only for one another. They stood on air, high above the heads of the many dogs and cats that raced back and forth in the hallway, barking and meowing and making a terrible commotion. They walked forward—eyes sparked, whiskers bristled, and backs arched— step by step toward one another. There was no floor or ground beneath them. They just continued on, walking through the air step by step, step by step, hissing and crying out insults. But though they continued to walk, they never did come any nearer to one another. A step, another step, on and on they came; but the distance between the two did not change.

And then Mittens saw the huge gray cat. His eyes were flashing yellow and his crooked tail was lashing from side to side. Mittens wanted to laugh at the silly tail but she was too afraid to laugh. She was even too afraid to move. What would the big cat do to the black and orange toms?

Surely if they knew that he was coming they would turn tail and run. But the orange and black cats did not even notice him. They did not see the gray cat approaching. Mittens tried to call to them but the meow stuck in her throat. She tried to run but her feet would not move. She didn't want to see what would happen when the gray cat reached the black and orange cats.

The gray cat reached the black cat. He did not stop. He did not even look at him. He just passed right on by. He's going for the orange cat, thought Mittens. She watched in petrified silence. The gray cat walked on, angrily, defiantly. He reached the orange cat and walked right on by. He did not even look at the orange cat. His yellow eyes did not waver, his tail continued to whip back and forth, and his ragged ear flopped awkwardly with each step. Then Mittens realized with horror that the mean gray cat was coming her way. Step by step he came, the yellow eyes getting nearer and brighter every minute. Down below the dogs still ran back and forth barking and howling. Cats still scampered and clawed and meowed; but Mittens could see only the gray cat as he came steadily toward her, walking through the air, his eyes glistening and his tail lashing angrily.

Mittens shrank back, but her feet still refused to move. She tried to cry out in fright but her throat wouldn't work. The gray cat was very near now; he was within striking distance. Mittens felt sure that at any moment she would feel the tear of his sharp claws and the pain of his strong teeth.

There was nothing. He was walking right on by as though he did not even see Mittens standing there. The yellow eyes did not even flicker; only the tail flipped back and forth, crazily thumping with each step that the large cat took.

Then Mittens was able to move. She felt herself sinking,

sinking,

and then she was awake—awake and trembling from head to foot. She still lay among her brothers and sister. Even Brother Number Three had joined them. He lay heavily on Mittens' hind quarters, pinning her to the wire mesh floor. Sister lay beside her, purring contentedly even as she slept. Mittens' head rested on the back of Brother Number Two. He still slept peacefully, even though that was all that he had been doing all day. Mittens let her eyes go hurriedly to the front of their cage. Yes, the wire mesh was still secure in its place, she noticed thankfully. The big gray cat would not be taking them by surprise. Mittens was still too frightened to move. She lay—trying to still her thumping heart—feeling at one and the same time both hot and cold.

Brother Number One stirred. "Where are those guys?" he complained. "Surely it must be time to eat by now."

Brother Number Two had awakened. "You're always hungry," he laughed. "We've just had our breakfast and here you are wantin' to eat again."

But Brother Number One was not in a good mood and not about to take teasing good naturedly. "How would you know what time it is?" he snapped back. "You've been sleeping all day."

Brother Number Two was not to be baited. He just yawned and stretched and pulled himself away from the huddle of kittens and went to get himself a drink, noisily lapping at the water spout. The sound made Mittens thirsty. She got up and went to fight for a position at the water jar too. Her thirstiness helped to drive away the lingering fright from her dream. She and Brother Number Two pushed and shoved at one another so that they might get their fill of the cool water. Brother Number Two was less aggressive than Mittens, even though he was bigger; and his easy-going disposition allowed her to get several good licks in before he shouldered her aside. Soon Brother Number Three had joined them. He pushed them both aside and helped himself. Mittens was content to let him take over. She had had enough for the present. Brother Number Two was not prepared to fight for water rights, either. He moved over and sat down to wash the few drops off his face. Mittens saw it as a wonderful opportunity to have some fun and threw herself at him. Immediately they were wrestling, thrashing this way and tumbling that. In the excitement of the game Mittens forgot all about her dream and the big gray tom who sat in the cage so nearby, his yellow eyes studying everything before him and his crooked tail lashing angrily back and forth.

Chapter 6

Neighbors

The green-coated people came again with their evening meal. Again there was an awful commotion. Only the black older dog and the little fluffy puppy did not join in all of the barking and meowing. The black dog pressed her nose against the wire mesh and let her tail wave back and forth as she waited contentedly. The little pup was far too busy romping and playing to be bothered. He only barked —an excited little *yip*—when he managed to catch his tail in his play, or a pain-filled sharp *yap* when he happened to bite down on it too hard with his little teeth.

Mittens deliberately kept her eyes from straying to the cage of the big gray cat. She didn't want to see the yellow eyes as they looked out coolly and disdainfully on the confined world. Instead, she looked on down the aisle at the two men as they moved along, filling dish after dish and pouring fresh water into the water jars.

Mittens watched as the one people-person stopped and playfully tousled the ear of the little pup who did stop playing long enough to dive into his dinner dish.

Mittens turned back to the two people-persons and

watched them as they fed the two toms. The cats did not look at one another. They were both meowing loudly, impatient for their food. They both wanted to be first. Mittens noticed that neither one of them was very polite. In fact, the black one even swiped at the hand of the people-person as the water jar was placed in the cage. The green-coated attendant jerked his hand back quickly, but he didn't seem at all surprised.

"Nearly got you that time," said the other man, and laughed a little bit.

"Don't laugh," said the first man. "It's your turn to feed him tomorrow."

They moved on. The one people-person fed the dog with the big feet and long floppy ears. Mittens watched. She wanted to see how he could eat with the ears dangling in his dish. To her amazement the man reached into his pocket and pulled out some funny-looking contraption and pinned the droopy ears up on the top of the dog's head. The dog ate hungrily, paying no attention to his new ear-do. Mittens called Sister over for a look. The two of them laughed together and then began a game of tag around the interior of the cage. They raced back to the front of the cage again and skidded to a stop. Mittens loved to play tag but she didn't want to miss anything that was going on in the hallway.

Sister still wanted to play, and when Mittens wouldn't join her she turned instead to Brother Number One. He wasn't the least bit interested in anything but his dinner. Sister then playfully pounced on Brother Number Two who was well rested up, and ready for a game. He darted after Sister, and the chase was on.

Mittens tried to ignore the two of them, but it was difficult. They seemed to be everywhere at once, running, jumping, dashing, and diving. Brother Number Three was bumped right off his feet. He decided not to complain but

to join in the game. Brother Number One could not resist and soon he too was racing with them. There wasn't much room for four kittens to run, so soon the game had changed from tag to a wrestling match. That pleased Mittens. At least she wasn't being constantly bumped and jumped over. Her eyes stayed fastened on the two people-persons and the food containers and water pails.

One of them had reached the quiet black dog. She pressed her nose even more closely against the wire. Her tail waved back and forth more quickly. A soft sound came from her throat. Yet her eyes were not on the dish of food but on the people-person. He reached a hand out and flipped a little door in the wire cage front. It swung open and he reached his hand in. The dog moved quickly to the extended hand, putting out a long tongue to caress it. The man patted the dog and spoke to her. She waved her tail faster and licked again at the hand. She was far more excited about the patting than she was about the dish of food.

Mittens watched and wondered. Why was the dog so eager to be touched by the green-frocked people-person? If he brought her dinner and her water, wasn't that enough? The man withdrew his hand and lifted in the dish of food. Then he refilled the water jar and patted the dog's head again, still talking to her. He shut the little door in the wire mesh front of the cage and moved on to the next cage with the thin cat. The second people-person was already busy working at the cage of the big gray tom. Mittens wanted to watch the thin cat receive her dinner but her eyes went instead to the big tom. If the black cat and the orange cat had been so ungracious, what would the gray cat be like, she wondered. But the gray cat did not growl nor swat at the feeding hand. Instead the gray cat pulled away from the door, just as far away as he could. The large body seemed to quiver, and he pressed himself against the far wall of the wire cage.

"It's okay, old man. I'm not going to hurt you," the green-coated attendant said; but the gray cat didn't seem to believe him. He backed into the far corner as far as he could, his tail still and his body trembling. Only after the door had been securely fastened and the men had moved on did the cat come slinking slowly forward, looking with darting yellow eyes from side to side. He sniffed cautiously at his dish and then, though he appeared not to wish to, he poked his whole big head into it and began to eat hungrily. Mittens could not take her eyes from him. Never had she seen a dish of food disappear so quickly.

The big gray tom backed away from the empty dish to his corner again. He licked his chops and cleaned his whiskers, all the time looking stealthily about with wild yellow eyes.

The men were working their way back down the aisle, feeding hungry and demanding animals as they came. Mittens was reminded about her own hungry and complaining stomach. It seemed that it was forever since she had had anything to eat. All of the kittens had stopped their game and joined her at the front of the cage. They were just as noisy as any of the other animals as they coaxed for their dinner.

One of the people-persons soon reached their cage and opened the little door. He reached in and all five kittens ran eagerly to his hand. He laughed as he pushed them aside and found room to set down their dish of dinner food. They all pressed toward it, forgetting the human hand that had presented it to them and thinking only of getting the food into their hungry tummies before the other family members ate it all.

There didn't seem to be much to do after finishing their meal. They cleaned their faces and paws and then played some, and soon it was time to curl up for bed again. Mittens didn't join the other kittens in their bed in the corner. She wanted to be there waiting when Cindy arrived. She sat at the front of the cage, her eyes on the aisle before her. All of the other kittens were sleeping—she could hear their soft breathing. Even the other animals in the cages nearby had settled down. Mittens looked out at her neighbors. The old dog had left her position from close to the mesh door. She was curled up now, still near the front of the wire cage but no longer standing. Her nose was tucked on her paws, and she slept peacefully. Even the puppy no longer played. He slept in a tumbled ball, looking as though he had fallen mid-jump, just too exhausted to continue his games any longer.

The black cat slept with one black foot extended, the claws slowly working. The orange cat slept too, but his head was turned as though he was listening for any sound of his neighbor even as he slept.

Mittens looked up and down the row of cages. All of the inhabitants seemed to be weary of the long day and only too willing to bring it to a close by shutting it out with sleep.

Only the big gray cat was not sleeping. He still sat at the front of his cage, his yellow eyes reflecting the light of the lamp hanging over their heads. As Mittens watched, he moved from his position and began to pace. Back and forth, back and forth, he walked—stopping now and again to sniff at the wire before him. And always as he walked, his crippled tail whipped this way and that behind him.

Still Cindy did not come. Mittens felt her eyes get heavier and heavier. She had wanted to be there ready and waiting when Cindy came in carrying the carrier box. She also longed to be curled up with her brothers and sister, feeling the warmth of their bodies as they slept together. She looked over at them now, wishing that she could go join them. Finally she lowered herself to the wire floor and rested her head on her paws. She was too tired to stand any longer. She would just have a little nap as she waited for

Cindy.

When Mittens awoke, it was a new day again. The noise in the "place of cages" told her that the other animals were already calling for their breakfast. Mittens opened her eyes and looked about her, wondering why she was sleeping alone. In the corner she saw her brothers and sister, and for a moment she could not understand why she was not with them. Then she remembered how she had fallen asleep while waiting for Cindy to come. They were all still there. Cindy had not come as she had expected. Surely Cindy would return for them on this day.

Mittens stood and stretched. She felt a little cold from sleeping all night without the warmth and comfort of her brothers and sister. She was tempted to go crawl in with them now; but before she could move to do so they began to stir, and soon all four of them were rising from their bed, stretching and awakening, ready to begin a new day.

"They're late again," complained Brother Number Three.

"Who're late?" asked Sister sleepily.

"The people-persons with the breakfast," said Brother.

"You just woke up," teased Brother Number Two. "How do you—"

But Brother Number Three cut in angrily. "How do I know they're late? Because my stomach tells me, that's how. That's not hard to figure, whether I just woke up or not. Any dummy—"

But there was a noise at the door and all five kittens ran to the front of the cage to see the two green coats with a cart loaded with dishes and jugs and boxes and bags.

Wild barking and meowing followed. It was so loud that Mittens could not even make Brother Number Two, who stood beside her, hear her words. She decided to wait until later to talk. Instead she began to watch as the two men moved down the aisle, stopping at each cage to fill dishes and jugs and clean the interior.

It seemed to take them a long time to get to the kittens. By then Mittens and her sister and brothers were just as noisy as all of the other dwellers. They accepted the food and water without a *thank you* and began again to hungrily gulp the food.

After breakfast there were more washings, more naps, and more games. Mittens wandered to the front of the cage now and then to look out curiously at the other inhabitants. They were behaving in the same manner that they had the day before. Mittens began to feel that she could have told anyone, at any time of day, just what any of the other animals would be doing. The pup would be playing his silly games all by himself; the black dog would be standing pressed near the front of her cage, her tail ever-wagging; the thin cat would be sitting, looking half-alive; the black and white dog would be standing, feet braced, barking at nothing; the black and orange cats would be glaring at one another; and the mother dog would be nursing her always-hungry puppies. Then, of course, there was the big gray cat. He would be sitting, staring straight ahead, his yellow eyes looking angry and defiant, his tail swishing back and forth at its crazy crooked angle, *flip-flop, flip-flop.*

Mittens yawned. It was all really very boring. There was never any change of the routine. At the people-house, there had been a variety of things to do. Here, in their small cage—empty of all but food dish and water jar—there was very little to catch one's attention. Mittens went back to the corner for another nap.

The day passed again. They played and napped intermittently. Mittens spent some time watching her neighbors, but still she was bored. She found herself wishing that she was sharing the cage with the active pup. he was the only one of them that seemed to be having any fun. Mittens knew that she was not supposed to even like dogs, but she thought that maybe this one could be an exception.

Well, there was no way for her to join the pup in his play, so there was really no use even thinking about it. She yawned again and went to chase Brother Number Two's tail. He seemed to be having a dream as he slept in the corner, for his tail moved gently back and forth every now and then. Mittens pounced upon it. That one action ended her game and also ended Brother Number Two's sleep. He awoke with a loud screech. Mittens had bitten too hard. She fled around the small cage, trying to keep out of the range of Brother's angry claws.

Brother Number Two soon forgot his anger, and the fight turned into play. They wrestled and tumbled, and then Brother Number Two forgot himself and closed his jaws too firmly over one of Mittens' paws. The play turned into a fight again.

It was the sound of the evening meal coming that broke it up. Suddenly they both realized just how hungry they were and rushed to join their brothers and their sister at the front of the cage, trying hard to make their mewing heard over the awful din of all of the other mewing and barking. It was useless, Mittens knew that; but she kept right on meowing loudly anyway.

Mittens had expected the routine to go just as it had at each mealtime. It started out that way. On down the line came the two green-coated men, stopping at each cage to open the small mesh door and reach in to give the new supply of food and the fresh water to each of the animals. None of the animals seemed grateful except for the old black dog. She always praised them extensively, pressing forward to lick the hands and receive the affectionate pats. Mittens licked her lips in anticipation. She didn't know if she was really hungry or just welcomed the food as something to do with her time.

Mittens watched as one people-person stopped at the cages of the black and orange toms. Before he opened the small door he stopped and pulled a glove over his hand. When he reached in the cage to feed the black cat, the cat's back came up with an angry arch and he hissed loudly. Then, quick as a flash, the paw darted out and slashed at the hand. The man jumped, in reflex action; but he was unharmed.

"Outsmarted you, cat," he said. "I have no intention of wearing your claw marks around for the rest of the week."

The cat was still angry. He sputtered and spit as his water jar was filled and replaced, but he did not strike again.

The man wore the glove to care for the orange cat as well. But though the orange cat was upset and cross about the intruding hand, it did not strike at the man.

Mittens watched as the two men moved on down the line. The black dog was patted again and whined softly after the man had left her. She did not even bother to try the food in her dish.

When one of the attendants came to the cage of the big gray tom, he opened the little door carefully.

"Out of water. I'll go get some more," said his companion and picked up the pail and started for the door.

The big gray had pressed himself against the far side of his cage. He stood trembling, his eyes darting here and there.

"You'd better report on this tabby too," the man at the gray's cage called after him. "I still don't like the way she looks. I don't think that she has gained an ounce since she came in here."

The first man came back a few steps, and both of the green-coated men stood looking at the thin half-grown cat in the cage next to the big gray.

"She doesn't look too good, does she? Thought that she

would have put on some weight by now. Maybe we should have the vet check her out tomorrow.''

"Write her number down in the book.''

The man picked up the pail again and continued to the door. The other man still looked at the tabby.

All of this time the big gray had been looking at the little open door. He pressed himself in the corner, his eyes gleaming, his tail twitching.

Suddenly, he made a lunge. His big body was just able to squeeze through the small opening. Right past the surprised man he flew, hitting the cement floor with a heavy *thud*. The man who was going for water had just opened the big door to go through it. The big gray streaked after him.

"Close the door!'' shouted the second green-coated man, as he began to run after the fleeing cat.

"What?'' the other man shouted back, turning to see what all of the commotion was about. By now all of the dogs in the place had stopped their eating and began barking in one wild, noisy chorus.

"Close the door!'' the man shouted again; but his words were lost in all of the other noise.

The first man saw the cat then, but it was too late. He made a leap to grab him before he slipped out the door but only succeeded in sprawling on the cement floor, his pail making a terrible clatter as he did so.

Both men were gone from the room for some time. It took ages for the dogs to settle down to their eating again. In between the barking of the dogs and the mewing of the cats that were still waiting impatiently for their dinner, Mittens could hear people-person voices. They seemed to be excited about something. Mittens expected to see them come back again with the gray tom tucked away in a carrier box; but when the men came back to resume feeding the other hungry animals, there was no carrier box and the big gray tom was not with them. The little mesh door of the

cage was not closed.

The next morning the cage across the way was thoroughly cleaned with some strange-smelling *something,* but the big gray tom did not come back to live in the cage again.

Chapter 7

A Visit to the Doctor

Mittens was all prepared for another boring day. Breakfast was served as usual. They washed, played, and then curled up for a nap. There didn't seem to be much happening since the big tom had made his escape. Mittens even tired of watching the puppy play. So, with nothing better to do, and feeling sleepy after her strenuous games with the other kittens, she snuggled close to them and fell asleep.

It seemed that she had just gotten to sleep when she felt a hand nuzzling her. For a moment she thought that Cindy must have come back, but then she quickly realized that the hand did not smell or feel like Cindy's hand. She forced her eyes open. She was lifted gently by a strange hand and placed in another carrier box. All of her brothers and her sister were placed in the same box; then they were on their way out of the room of many cages. As the door closed behind them, the noise faded away. Mittens found it strange to be suddenly free from bursts of sound.

They were carried to another room. This one was bright and Mittens blinked her eyes, unaccustomed to the glare that confronted them. When her eyes adjusted to the light, she was amazed to see that the sun had returned again. The wet was gone. She had been right. After the wet went away, the sun had come back again. Mittens was so glad to see the sun that she wanted to run and leap. But there was no room in the little carrier box for leaping and running.

The next thing that Mittens noticed was the strange smell. She didn't like it. She didn't like it at all. Her brothers and sister didn't seem to like it either. Brother Number Three began to cough and sneeze. Mittens could tell that he was angry at being taken into a room with such an unpleasant odor. He backed into a corner of the box, his back bristling and his eyes flashing.

"What next?" he said angrily. "First that stuffy box of Cindy's, then the room with all of the mad dogs and wire cages, and now this."

"At least we are in the sun again," said Sister, and Mittens wondered if Sister had been missing the sun as much as she had been missing it.

But Brother Number Three was not even comforted by that fact. "What good is the sun when you are stuffed together into this little space, forced to smell all of those vile—?" But he got no farther, for a hand was reaching into their box. They all backed away from it—all that is except Brother Number Two. He was already sleeping and was totally unaware of his surroundings or the reaching hand. The hand found him and lifted him out.

He was taken away and the rest of them remained where they were, wondering whatever was to become of him— and what was ever to become of them. It wasn't long until he was returned again. He was upset and in pain. They had taken him to a man in a white coat who had poked and felt and looked him over from tip to tail, he said. Before he was even finished telling all about it, the hand reached in again; and though they all backed away from it, Brother Number One was picked up and carried away.

Brother Number Two continued his story. They had forced open his mouth and looked down his throat and picked at his teeth and poked something in his ears and shined a bright light in his eyes, he said. They had felt all of his bones and tested his muscular reaction, twisted his head this way and that, and then poked him with a sharp needle. He said that he hurt all over and didn't even want to talk about it. He crawled off to the far corner of the crowded box and went to sleep.

They all waited for Brother Number One to return. The time seemed to drag by. Mittens was getting thirsty. It was warm in the small carrier box. She even found the sunshine too bright for her eyes. She wished that she could sleep like Brother Number Two, but she didn't dare fall asleep for fear that the hand would reach in again and she would be the one taken. But when Brother Number One was returned to the box, it was Sister who was taken next.

Brother Number One had the same report as Brother Number Two. Brother Number Three snarled. "They'd never take me like that," he declared hotly. What right have they to take us off, one by one, and handle and poke us? I'll fight it," he said. "I'll fight it."

They waited for the return of Sister, but she did not come back to the box. The hand came again though, and Mittens was the next one to be lifted out. She wanted to fight the hand too for she was frightened by now. Frightened because of what Brothers Number One and Two had said. Frightened because Sister had not been returned to the box. Frightened because of the awful smell in this strange place. She tried to twist herself free, but the hands held her securely.

It was a strange place where the hands carried her. They passed her over to another pair of hands which were gentle and accompanied by a kind voice. Mittens saw the long white coat and knew that she was being handled by the

same person who had handled her brothers. She wanted to scratch at the pair of hands but was held in such a manner that she couldn't get her claws in an effective scratching position.

The voice continued to speak to her and the hands continued to stroke her soft fur. She could feel the fear beginning to drain from her. Then she was placed on a strange white table and the hands began to pass over her body, checking every inch of her. It was just as Brother had said. They shone the light into her eyes and pushed something into her ears. They opened her mouth and checked her small white teeth and they held down her tongue as they looked at her throat. Mittens tried to struggle free but was unable to move. Then she felt it—the sharp sting of the needle. It smarted as it broke through the skin and stung in her hip for a brief period of time.

The next thing that Mittens knew she was waking up from a bleary sleep. Her head seemed heavy and her eyes wouldn't focus right. Her throat felt dry and hot, and she longed for a drink of water. She tried hard to concentrate on where she was and what had happened, and then she remembered being carried in the carrier box with her brothers and sister to the strange-smelling room with the bright sunshine streaming in the window.

She tried to get to her feet but she felt shaky. There were parts of her body that hurt. She tried to remember just what had happened to her. *Oh, yes. The needle.* That was the last thing that she remembered. *Where am I now? Am I still in the room with the high white table?* No, she could see that she was not. Nor was she back in the room with the long line of cages. *Am I back, then, with my brothers and sister in the carrier box?* No, she had not been returned to the carrier box either, for the place where she was lying had far more room than that. Then where was she? And why was she all alone?

Before Mittens could get her bearings, a pair of hands was again lifting her.

"Hello, Sweetie," a voice was saying, as the hands gently lifted her from wherever she was. "Let's have a little warm milk. Are you wide enough awake yet?"

Mittens was still afraid of the hands, though they felt gentle enough. But she remembered that the other pair of hands had felt gentle too, and yet she ached all over after her experience with them. Was it the hands or the strange smell that had caused her soreness? Somehow the smell seemed to be a very real part of it all. She let the hands lift her and stroke her gently.

"Let's get that milk now," the voice went on, and Mittens felt the warm milk as it trickled down her throat. At first she felt like she wouldn't be able to swallow, but she tried hard and her throat still worked. She swallowed again and again.

"Good girl," the voice crooned. "Good girl. That's what you need. Some nice warm milk to make you feel fine again."

Mittens took more of the milk. It helped her aching throat and filled her empty tummy. Her eyes began to focus better and she felt some strength returning to her weak legs.

"That's the girl," the voice said. "You'll be your old self in no time." Mittens doubted that, but she was feeling much better.

"I think that you are pretty well awake now," said the voice.

The hands picked her up gently and began to carry her along to somewhere. Mittens was aware enough now to wonder where her brothers and sister were. Why was she not with them? She had left her brothers in the carrier box in the bright room. Was her sister back in the box now too? Were the hands taking her back to join them? Mittens hoped so, for she missed her family.

It was not to the bright room that the hands carried Mittens. It was to another room entirely. This room was very small. It had a window that looked out to the outside world. Mittens was surprised to see that the sun was no longer shining brightly. Nor was there any wet out there, so the wet had not been responsible for driving the sun away. The sun was not shining simply because it was the time of the darkness. Mittens was used to getting ready for bed at this time of the day, and here she was just waking up from a very strange kind of sleep.

"Here you are now," said the voice. "In you go." And Mittens was being placed in another cage. This one had a very soft floor made of something that a cat could snuggle into instead of a wire floor like the cages in the other room.

Mittens liked the comfort but she still felt lonesome. She nosed around; something about the cage smelled familiar. Mittens sniffed harder, walking toward the welcoming smell. Her nose pushed up against a soft body lying curled up in a corner. It was Sister. Mittens nudged her in excitement, and Sister wakened from her drowsy sleep.

"You're here," said Mittens. "I wondered where they had taken you."

Mittens didn't wait for Sister's reply. She pushed on excitedly, expecting to find her brothers.

"Where are the boys?" she asked, when her nose told her that they weren't there.

"I don't know," said Sister. "I haven't seen them. But I am so glad to see you. I was all alone and—"

"Well, I'm here now," cut in Mittens, "and they will bring the boys soon, I'm sure."

"I hope so," said Sister. "I hated being without all of you. I was going to wait for all of you to come, but I was so sleepy I—"

"I know," said Mittens. "I'm sleepy too. Why, I must

have slept nearly half the day and I still feel—" But she couldn't go on. Her eyes were so heavy and her brain so fuzzy. She flopped down wearily beside Sister and let her head rest on the small soft body.

"I'm so glad you're here," Sister said sleepily. "When the boys—" But she was just too sleepy to go on.

Mittens attempted an answer but it never did come. She was asleep again before she could utter it. They slept together, curled up closely, each one taking comfort from the other. They still hurt from their visit to the man in the white coat, but they would feel much better tomorrow. In the meantime, they had one another; and they were sure that their brothers would soon be back with them as well. For the moment all that they really needed was more sleep.

Chapter 8

Moving Again

Mittens was still sore when she awoke the next morning—sore and very hungry. As she watched Sister crawl out of bed and begin her grooming, she knew that she must be sore as well. She could tell by the way that she moved about.

Breakfast soon came. They ate quickly at first and then remembered that there were no longer five of them to eat from the one dish. Not needing to fear that they wouldn't get their fair share, they slowed down and enjoyed the food a bit more. It seemed strange not to be pushed and shoved and rushed as one ate breakfast.

After breakfast they both cared for their grooming. They moved about rather slowly and didn't feel much like playing. Mittens sat and looked about her after she had finished washing her coat. There really wasn't much to see. No cages full of other animals lined the walls of this room. There were two other box-rooms like the one that they were in; but as far as Mittens could see, they were both empty. It didn't promise to be a very exciting day. They curled up in the corner and slept again.

The day passed by again. They were fed and bedded.
The next day, as they came from their bed to welcome their
breakfast, they both felt much better. Mittens still wasn't
sure that she was ready to play, but she wasn't hurting
nearly as much any more. Sister looked spunkier too. She
spent the usual time on her grooming. She had been rather
neglectful the past two days and had some catching up to
do.

Mittens watched her because there was nothing else to
do. Again she marvelled that a cat as small as Sister could
spend so much time cleaning such a tiny bit of fur.

The door opened and two people-persons, both in white
coats, came into the room. One of them was carrying the
thin black cat. She looked sleepy, and on her side was a
strange looking white patch.

The man-person spoke. "I think that she came through
it rather well. Without that tumor she should be able to
pick up quickly, if she has no complications. We'll still
have to keep her quiet for a few days yet, but she seems to
be doing very nicely."

The woman-person, who was carrying the bandaged cat,
seemed to agree. "I've been watching her closely for the
past twenty-four hours," she said, "and she seems to be
doing fine."

They put the cat in one of the other boxes and then went
over to look at Mittens and Sister.

"Well, looky here; but aren't you looking chipper
today?" said the man-person, reaching in a hand.

The kittens both backed away, not quite trusting the
hand, even though the intention seemed to be kindness.
Sister's back even went up.

The man laughed and cornered Mittens and lifted her
from the small cage-box.

"It's okay," he said. "You are almost as good as new.
No, even better than new. With a couple more shots, you

will make some little girl very happy.''

Mittens didn't know what he was talking about. Cindy was the only little girl that she knew; and, to be honest, she had almost forgotten what she looked like. It now seemed like a long time since she had seen Cindy. Maybe Cindy was coming back to get the kittens again. Mittens suddenly realized that she didn't really care any more. She still didn't like the smelly room that they were in. She would just as soon go back to where all of the animals were kept. At least there was something to watch there—not much, but something.

"Do you want them taken out?" the woman-person asked.

"We'll wait until tomorrow."

The man-person was stroking Mittens' ear. It felt good, but she still didn't trust him. She looked around her for a high white table, but didn't see one. Still, she decided, he might not need a high table to begin his picking and poking. She feared lest the pricking needle would appear out of nowhere in his hand again.

The man-person put her back down in the cage-box without so much as one pinch or poke. Mittens nearly went crazy with relief. She dashed over to Sister who stood in the far corner with her back ready to go up at the slightest move toward her. She was glad to see Mittens, too, and they rocked back and forth together.

"Look at that," the man-person laughed.

"They are really cute little rascals," agreed the woman-person. "We won't have any trouble at all finding them homes. I'd like to take them myself."

"You—" laughed the man more heartily, "you'd take every animal in here."

The woman laughed with him. "Not quite," she said. "You couldn't get me near that black tom, or the orange one either for that matter."

"They are a bit fiesty, aren't they?"

"A bit? That's putting it mildly. I don't think that we'll ever get them to the place where they will be able to go to a home."

"We'll give them another week. If there's no change, we'll just have to put them to sleep."

"I hate to see that. They really are pretty cats—both of them."

"Well, we can't go on feeding them forever."

The two people-persons walked out. Mittens and Sister both stood watching them go. Through the open door streamed the sunshine. Mittens longed to be out in it. She could almost feel the warmth of the rays on her back. Then the door swung shut again and they were left with only the ceiling light to shine down upon them. Mittens looked up at it and a feeling of disgust filled her. There was no kind warmth from the lamp above. It wasn't at all like the sun. Well, she still had Sister; there was warmth there. They curled up together and continued their nap.

They hadn't been sleeping long when there was more movement in the room that wakened them. Two people-persons were at the cage of the thin cat, bending over her. One was the woman-person in the white coat and the other was one of the green-coated men-persons.

"She has a fever," said the woman. "I don't like it."

"She never has been strong," said the man.

"I don't like the feel of this area around the incision either. She might have to go back to surgery."

"Do you think that she can stand another trip?"

"I don't think there is much choice. She won't get better like she is."

"I'll tell Doc. How soon do you want it set up?"

"The sooner the better. I'll take her to the examining room and see what I can find out."

The thin cat was lifted gently and placed in a funny little carrier box. She did not even waken.

Mittens and Sister watched the strange procession as it left the little room. Mittens supposed that they would never see the thin cat again.

It wasn't until the next morning that the cat was brought back to the room. She still looked sleepy. She was fed a little milk from a funny little bottle. Mittens and Sister both stood and watched as the white-coated people-person worked over her.

"I think that she'll make it now," she said to the green-smocked man who stood with her. "She had some internal bleeding, but we were able to do the necessary repair."

"She'll be a pretty cat when she gets on her feet."

"I don't think that we'll have any trouble placing her at all. I wouldn't mind taking her myself."

The green-coated man laughed. Apparently he had heard the words before from the white-frocked woman-person.

They left the room after a few minutes, and Mittens and Sister sat watching the bed of the thin cat. She continued to sleep and did not so much as stretch or work a claw as she did. It got to be boring, so Mittens leaped upon her sister to get a game going.

They were in the thick of it when the green-coated man-person appeared.

Before they could even untangle themselves, they were both being lifted out of the cage-box. They were not placed in a carrier box but were carried in the man's strong but kind hands.

He took them back out through the room filled with sunshine and on through to another room.

"Here they are," he said to the woman in the white coat. "What a display they will make."

The woman smiled. "They should draw a crowd all right," she agreed.

She reached out a hand to caress each kitten on her soft back. "Everything ready for them?"

"All set."

"In they go then."

The man moved on, and they found themselves in a new box-cage. This one was bigger than they were used to. It was glass on three sides so that they could see out. There was no sun, but there were bright lights shining down from way, way above their heads. There was a water jar there and a food dish and lots and lots of newspaper to play and sleep in. It was a strange place, but Mittens liked it almost immediately. Sister wasn't so sure. She looked around nervously; she felt so exposed. All around were bright lights and milling people-persons. How would one ever get any sleep in such a place?

Mittens did not concern herself with things like sleep. She liked to be where she could see action, and this looked like a perfect place for that.

"Oh, come on," she said to her sister, giving her a play- ful push. "Don't be so gloomy. Look on the bright side. Just see all of the things that there are to look at."

Sister pushed back, but she didn't seem to be feeling very playful. A loud squawk caught their attention, and both of them raised their heads. Very near them, sitting on an open perch, was a large colorful bird. Mittens had never seen such bright feathers. He squawked again and Mittens marvelled at the bigness of his mouth. He was a cocky fellow. Mittens thought about how much fun it would be to chase him and put him to flight. A young people-person came near him and poked at him with a finger.

"Don't touch the bird," a big people-person said. "See the sign? He bites."

The big people-person walked away with another people-

person to look at some small cans that were stacked on a shelf and the little people-person watched him go. He looked back at the bird again and then back at the man-person, who had his back to the bird.

The young people-person reached out his hand again and poked at the bird. With lightning speed, the big bird clamped down hard on the outstretched finger. The young boy jumped back—but not quickly enough. The bird caught the finger in his strong beak. The boy started to cry out but checked himself. He looked over at the big man-person. He still had his back to the boy. The young people-person put his hand into his pocket and hurried from the store. As he went by the kittens, Mittens could see tears in his eyes, but his hand stayed in his pocket.

The big bird was chuckling to himself. It delighted him that he had put the boy on the run.

"You shouldn't have done that," said a raspy voice.

Mittens looked over and saw another bird on a perch near the colorful fellow. She had not noticed him there before. His feathers were all white.

"Why not?" still chuckled the big fellow. "He asked for it. I get tired of their poking."

"He didn't mean any harm."

"Well, he won't try it again either, I'll just bet you."

"Oh, yeah? The next time, he will use a stick or some sharp-pointed object and then *you* will be the one smarting."

The colorful bird clicked his beak and said some very unwise words. The white one turned his back on him and moved to the far end of the perch.

Mittens had rather enjoyed watching the whole thing, but when things seemed to quiet down again she went back to tumbling in the newspaper.

A number of people-persons gathered around and said many strange things about the kittens. Neither Mittens nor Sister could understand their talk, but then neither of them

were particularly interested in it either. They were much too busy playing to be bothered.

Now this, thought Mittens, *is the best place that we've been yet. I really like it here. I hope that they don't move us again.*

Mittens had barely finished the thought when she was being lifted again.

"Here we go again," she said to her sister. "Can't they leave us any place for more than a few hours?"

But the hands that lifted Mittens did not reach in again for Sister. Mittens thought it strange, but hoped that it meant that she, too, would soon be placed back in the cage again.

Instead she was passed to the hands of a little girl-person. The hands smelled of ice cream and, for the moment, Mittens forgot everything but trying to get a little of the second-hand treat. She began to lick at the hands. The little girl squealed her delight.

"Is that the one you want?" asked the woman-person standing beside her.

The little girl said nothing but nodded her head vigorously.

"Are you sure?"

She nodded again.

"Well, say something."

The little girl looked up. "Yes—thank you," she said politely.

"That's much better," said the big people-person. Then she turned to the people-person in the green coat. "How much is she?" she asked.

They talked and Mittens licked. The ice cream all seemed to be gone but she still kept licking, hoping that she would discover some more.

"Hold her tightly now," the big woman people-person was saying. "We don't want her to get away."

The little girl held Mittens so tightly that she felt all of the breath go out of her. She wriggled and was held even tighter.

"Here," said the big person, bending over both of them. "Hold her like this. Firmly but not uncomfortably."

The little girl shifted her hands. It felt much better to Mittens.

They passed out of the store. Mittens thought that they would stop at the big glass cage, and she would be placed back in beside Sister again, but the little girl walked right by. There stood Sister, looking forlornly out, watching Mittens being carried away. Mittens did not even have the chance to call out to her.

Chapter 9

A New Home

"Dorothy," said the big people-person, "don't hold your kitty too tightly."

They were in another big monster hurrying through the streets. This one was red in color, instead of blue like the one Cindy's family was always gobbled up by; so Mittens did not expect to end up back at Cindy's house. Where they were going she had no idea. It seemed that she had done a good deal of moving in the last while. She hated to leave the glass cage with its high ceiling and interesting people-persons to watch. Maybe these people would take her back soon. But Mittens had her doubts. As she thought back over the past few days, she could not remember returning to any of the places that she had been.

Soon the big red monster-thing was stopping and they were getting out. Dorothy—as the mother-person called the young girl-person—carried Mittens in to a house with brick walls and white shutters. It looked like a cozy place—for people—thought Mittens. It was too plain and uninteresting to her. When Dorothy opened the door and went in, she was greeted with wild yipping. A dog had

somehow gotten into the house. Mittens tried to wriggle free and get out of the reach of the dog. Dorothy held her even tighter. Mittens meowed and struggled harder.

"Now, be good," said Dorothy.

Mittens replied that things would be fine as soon as the dog was chased out where he belonged, but Dorothy didn't seem to understand her.

"Here," she said, lowering Mittens into dangerous range of the dog. "I want you two to be friends."

The dog thrust a nose out to sniff at Mittens. Mittens let out a *yowl* and struck with all the force of her small paw. The dog jerked back with a cry of pain. There was anger in his voice as he protested. Mittens gave another lurch in Dorothy's arms and sprang free. Dorothy tried to grab her, but she sailed right over the reaching hands and landed firmly on her four kitten feet. The dog forgot his anger and made a jump after her. Mittens could sense that she didn't have a minute to lose. She moved forward with lightning speed and headed for some furniture for cover. The dog was right behind her. Mittens ran under a chair, but the dog was small enough that he could run under the chair too.

Mittens ran for the couch. The dog came squeezing behind the couch too.

Mittens thought of bedrooms. Usually there was a dresser that was too close to the floor to accommodate even small dogs. She headed for the nearest door.

It was not a bedroom. It was a study. A big man-person sat at a desk working with many papers spread out before him. There didn't seem to be anything to go under, so Mittens decided to go over. Up and over the desk she went, scattering the papers in all directions. The big man-person was yelling after her but she ran on.

She skidded around the corner, slipped on the shiny floor, and looked for another door. The dog was still right behind her. Mittens heard a loud crash as something came tumbling down from somewhere; but as she ran, she did not even turn her head to check on what it was and where it had come from. On she ran, the dog yipping and yapping close on her heels. After the dog came the girl-person Dorothy, and after Dorothy came the mother-person. Mittens did not look to see if the man-person had joined them as well; the dog was too close upon her heels for her to take the time.

The next room that Mittens dashed into was a bathroom. There was nothing to hide under, so again Mittens leaped up. She stood on the vanity, her back arched, her lips drawn back in a snarl. The dog leaped and jumped below her, but he was not as agile as a cat. Mittens moved carefully forward and took a swipe at him with her outstretched claws. She caught his nose and he fell back with a loud cry; and then he came right back again, leaping and jumping some more. Mittens moved to take another slash at him as something beside her went crashing to the floor.

Dorothy reached the room. She was puffing from all of the running.

"Stop it," she shouted. "Look what you've done."

The room was beginning to smell very strange. Whatever it was that had fallen and broken seemed to smell a lot.

"Mama's favorite cologne," said Dorothy. "She's gonna be mad."

But Mittens did not wait to talk it over with Dorothy's mother. She saw a chance to make a dive for the door and she took it. Right past Dorothy and the startled dog she went, up and over and out; and when she landed on the slippery floor, she was already running.

The next door was a bedroom and Mittens found a dresser under which she could be safe. She hated to have the dog sniffing at the edge of it, but she would not even dare get close enough to him to slap him on his already

bleeding nose.

Dorothy came in and called to Mittens, but Mittens would not move. The mother-person came in too and told Dorothy to take "Taffy" out. Dorothy left with the dog. The dog didn't want to go. He seemed to feel that he could still get the better of the kitten if he was just given another chance. Dorothy carried him, still complaining, from the room.

Mittens stayed right where she was. She could still smell and hear the dog in the house, and she had no intention of coming out until they got rid of him. Dorothy came in now and then and coaxed her to leave the safety of the dresser, but Mittens would not respond.

It was getting late and still Mittens had not moved. She was hungry and cramped, but she felt much safer where she was than sharing the close quarters of a house with a dog.

Dorothy came in again and tried to coax her out with a dish of food. Mittens was hungry but she still wouldn't move. Dorothy took the handle of some kind of broom and tried to force Mittens out. Mittens stepped over the broom and backed into a far corner.

"I don't even think you got a cat," said a boy-person voice.

"I do too. Mama let me get her today, and if your dumb ole dog hadn't scared her so bad—"

"Don't call Taffy a dumb ole dog. It was *your* cat that broke the vase and the cologne—"

"She wouldn't have, if *your* dog hadn't been chasing her."

"Children," said the mother-person's voice. "Stop your quarreling."

"She won't come out," whined Dorothy.

"She's had an awful scare."

"But she must be hungry."

"When she gets hungry enough, she'll come out."

"But what will we do?"

"Let her starve," said the boy.

"Peter," said the mother-person, "it's time for you to go to bed."

"Aw—. I wanted to see her."

"In the morning," the mother said firmly.

"Dumb ole cat," the boy-person mumbled as he left the room.

"What will I do, Mother?" asked the girl. "She must be awfully thirsty and hungry by now."

"Just leave the food and the water here for her. When she gets hungry and thirsty enough, she will come out for it."

"She's still scared of Taffy."

"Well, keep your door closed tightly. Now get ready for bed."

"Can't I just stay up and watch for a while?"

"No. It's bedtime. Besides, watching isn't going to do any good. Now, to bed. Quickly."

The mother-person went out and closed the door tightly. Dorothy began to get ready for bed as she had been told.

Mittens could smell the water and food. It was making her throat dry and her stomach growl. She wanted to go out to it but she was still afraid. Once, she had almost convinced herself that it would be safe, when she smelled the dog smell very strongly and then heard him sniffing at the door. She quickly changed her mind and backed more tightly into the corner.

The light went out, and Dorothy crawled into bed. Mittens crouched in the darkness. There were still noises coming from the other part of the house. Mittens knew that the big people-persons had not yet gone to their bedrooms. Maybe the dog was still up too. She waited.

After what seemed like hours, the house was totally

quiet. Mittens still waited, straining to catch any sound that might come her way, but there was nothing. Carefully she pushed her nose out from under the dresser and sniffed. The dog smell was not strong any more. Mittens dared to push forward a bit farther. Nothing happened. She stretched out her nose toward the water dish. She could not reach it without coming all of the way out. Carefully she came forward, pressing herself as close to the carpet as she could. Nothing happened. Nothing in the room moved.

Mittens arched her body to escape completely from under the low dresser. She still held her crouched position. She could reach the water now and she pushed in her nose and drank thirstily. There wasn't much room for food after Mittens had finished drinking. Still, she ate what she could and then washed herself carefully, as she had been taught. She looked at the closed door and felt quite safe. She decided to look about the room and see what she might find that was of interest.

There didn't seem to be all that much that a cat would care about. Certainly she found no other cats nor any indication that one had ever been there. Mittens decided that she was the first cat that had occupied this house. It wouldn't be too bad a place, once they got rid of the dog. Mittens was feeling tired, so she decided to look for a place to sleep.

Some of Dorothy's clothing was laying on a chair, so Mittens jumped up and made herself comfortable. There was no warmth there, though and Mittens suddenly missed Sister very much. She had never slept alone before and she didn't like it. Why hadn't these people taken her back to Sister or brought Sister along with her?

Mittens tried to sleep but she couldn't find a comfortable way to lay. She twisted and turned and nothing seemed to work. She just couldn't find a way to be warm and cozy.

At last she decided that she would try Dorothy's bed. Dorothy didn't seem to have any trouble sleeping. Mittens dropped softly to the floor and walked the few steps to Dorothy's bed. She leaped silently up beside the sleeping Dorothy and snuggled down close to her. The warmth from Dorothy was comforting and Mittens curled up and closed her eyes. At last she felt that she was ready for a much-needed rest. There were still a number of things that she couldn't understand or didn't like but she would try to sort them all out on the morrow.

Chapter 10

Calico

Mittens didn't go back to the strange place to join Sister or the brothers the next day, or the next, or the next. She soon forgot to worry about it and settled down quite well in Dorothy's house.

There were some things that still bothered her. Her biggest worry was, of course, the dog. It wasn't long until Mittens realized that the family had absolutely no intention of getting rid of him. He was always with the boy-person when the boy was around, but the boy was gone most of the day and then the dog seemed to be everywhere.

Mittens soon learned to avoid him. She spent a good deal of her time under the dresser in Dorothy's room. Dorothy often shut the door, so that the dog couldn't get in and that left Mittens free to roam about the room at will. A litter box was kept in the room also, as well as one dish of water and one of food. So, except for being bored, Mittens was quite comfortable there. She did miss Dorothy in the big bed when she had her afternoon naps but she managed quite well.

The other thing that bothered Mittens was her name.

Dorothy didn't seem to know that Mittens already had a name, and had settled on a new one for her. It took Mittens some time to learn that when Dorothy went about calling "Calico," she, Mittens, was supposed to respond. Mittens didn't really care for the name Calico but Dorothy seemed to be quite pleased with it, so Mittens had to adjust too.

I guess that I am just Calico now, whether I want to be or not, thought Mittens—er, Calico. She wondered how Dorothy would feel if people began suddenly to call her "Topsy" or "Virginia."

The days went by—peacefully, for the most part. The dog and the cat were generally kept apart, for they had still not learned to live together in harmony. Calico had the deep feeling that Peter might have secretly enjoyed a good cat-dog fight but he never was given the opportunity to let one transpire.

Calico grew and added weight to her slim frame. She was sleek and pretty, and people-persons who visited the parents of Dorothy often fussed over her. She became very proud. She strutted about the house letting her arrogance show. The boy, Peter, might love his scruffy dog, but Calico had never seen anyone else making any kind of a fuss over the beast.

Calico had just decided that the world was a pretty neat place to be when something happened that shook her up again.

She was used to going with Dorothy in the big red monster, known now as the "car." She even enjoyed the trips. The most amazing thing about it was that they always came right back home again—back to the very place that they had started from. Calico was now convinced that she would never need to move again.

One day she heard Dorothy calling, "Calico, Calico."

Calico left her warm place in the sum and went running,

for Dorothy usually had something good to share when she called in such a way. Calico was not hungry nor was she thirsty. She had been fed and watered and her coat had been brushed. But she was spoiled and pampered, so she decided that if there was any good thing coming her way, she might as well take advantage of it. She hurried to Dorothy and was scooped up in her arms. There was no special treat waiting in Dorothy's hand, but the stroking felt good and Calico settled into a soft purr.

"You want to go for a car ride?" asked Dorothy. By now Calico knew what a car ride was and she also knew that she liked them. Besides, the dog, Taffy, never got to go with them when she went out with Dorothy and her mother in the car. Taffy only went when the boy went with the father.

Calico purred that a car ride would be just fine.

They left the house and drove through the streets in the bright afternoon sunshine. Dorothy wanted to hold Calico but Calico wanted to be up in the back window where she could see. They had a brief spat about it, and Calico won. She climbed up into the back window and gazed out at all of the interesting things that she passed.

It wasn't long until they were stopping. Dorothy reached for Calico and this time she would not accept her argument.

"Now be good," she scolded. "This won't take long."

She held Calico firmly and carried her into a building. To Calico's amazement, she found herself right back in the same building where she had been brought by Cindy so many months before.

"So you've brought your kitten in for her shot," said the people-person behind the desk. "She has really turned into a pretty thing, hasn't she?"

"I think so," beamed Dorothy. "She's the prettiest cat ever."

"The doctor will be with you in just a moment."

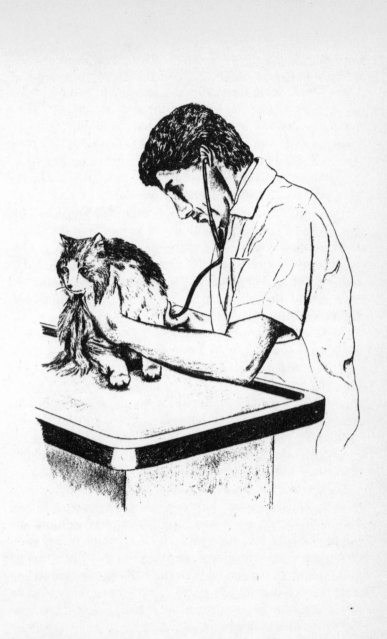

Calico looked around her. There were other people-persons in the room, many of them with animals. Some of them held them in their arms and some had them on leashes or in cages. Calico was glad that she wasn't caged up. There would be no way to escape then. She knew that from experience, and she had no intention of staying in this place again. She hated the smell. She hated the cages. She hated the other animals that she would have to share it with. She readied herself to make a dash for the door at the first opportunity. The chance did not come, for Dorothy held her firmly, all of the time talking to her softly and stroking the glistening coat.

Dorothy's name was called and she got up and moved to another room. There was the high, white table again, and there stood the very same man in the long white coat. Calico couldn't believe her eyes.

The man took the cat from Dorothy.

"Shot time again, huh? I'm glad that you didn't forget."

"I marked it on the calendar like you told me," said Dorothy.

"Good for you," answered the man. "It's very important that they have their shots if you want to keep them healthy."

"Well, I do," said Dorothy, with feeling. "I wouldn't want anything to happen to Calico."

"She's nice, isn't she?" All the time that the man was talking, his hands were carefully going over all of Calico's bones. She knew what was coming next. He would shine the bright light into her eyes, poke something in her ears, and force open her mouth so he could push her tongue around and shove something at her throat and jab at her teeth. Calico did not like the idea. She tensed herself to be ready to jump, but the doctor never once lessened his grip.

The needle came next. Calico felt the sting of it. She let out a yowl in protest. What business did they have to be picking and poking at the prettiest cat around? The doctor didn't seem to put much stock in prettiness.

Calico was sure that the next thing she would know, would be coming out of a hazy sleep and finding herself in some little cage-box in some back room. She wondered if Sister would still be there. But, to Calico's surprise, she was handed back to Dorothy, who carried her from the small room, her shoulder still stinging, and out to the waiting people-persons in the big room.

"We're ready," Dorothy said to her mother, and the mother got up and they all went back to the big red car and crawled in.

Calico was not interested in looking out. She crawled down into the depth of Dorothy's small lap and licked at her smarting shoulder. Something was going around and around in her brain. There was something wrong here. Things had no longer gone according to pattern. Always before when she had gone out in this car she was taken straight back home again. This time it had not been so. Before, when she had been taken to the place with the many lights, she had been put in a room with many cages. This time she had not seen that room. Before when she had visited the doctor, she had been given a needle and afterward slept a dizzy sleep. This time the needle had only smarted. They had not left her in the place of lights. Here she was on Dorothy's lap in the big car again. The pattern had stopped, and Calico wasn't sure just what could be trusted anymore. Perhaps she should not come running every time that Dorothy called. Certainly the experience of this day was not one she wished to repeat. Calico decided that from now on she would be a bit more cautious. Apparently the shaggy dog was not the only one in Dorothy's household who could not be totally trusted.

Chapter 11

The Picnic

Calico walked around for the next several days with a chip on her shoulder. She couldn't quite forgive Dorothy for tricking her with the car ride. After all why should *she* —such a pretty cat—be subject to such use and abuse? She scorned Dorothy's hands when they wished to caress her. Calico was torn between two emotions. She loved to be petted and stroked, but she didn't want to give Dorothy the pleasure of stroking her. So Calico denied herself, in order to deny her mistress.

She accepted all goodies but without gratitude. She came when called only if she wished to, and then she often turned and left again if she did not see evidence of something for her pleasure.

She still slept in Dorothy's bed, but she always waited until she knew that the girl was asleep. She did not want Dorothy to enjoy her presence, but she did want the comfort of Dorothy's warmth. When Dorothy would carry Calico and deposit her on the bed, inviting her to share the warmth and softness of the bed with her, Calico would always look about with disdain and quickly jump to the floor and squeeze herself back under the dresser. It was a tight fit now, for Calico was no longer the small kitten that she had been when she first came to the household.

Calico refused to make peace with Taffy. In fact, she discovered that there were ways to get the dog into a great deal of trouble. Whenever Taffy came around, even if he ignored Calico as he was sometimes prone to do now, Calico would bound up to the top of the highest piece of furniture that she could spot. Then she would brush heavily against something, in the hopes that she could make it topple. It most always worked. She found that that, accompanied by a great deal of wild meowing, almost always got Taffy sentenced to the back yard.

Calico didn't care for the back yard herself. She didn't like to get her shiny coat dirty. She didn't like the feel of cold or the ruffling of wind; and she absolutely hated the wet. The sun was nice, but she could feel it through the glass of the window, so why go outside for that? The birds were rather interesting but Calico no longer had the urge to play as she had at one time, and she had never even considered the birds in place of her ever-present cat dish and its variety of food. Calico was a very picky eater and was known, on many occasions, to turn her nose up at what she was offered and walk away.

So the back yard really had no appeal to her, and she was more than happy to leave it entirely to the dog.

Calico spent her days primping and fussing, sleeping and complaining, teasing and condemning. In spite of all of her faults, Dorothy loved her devotedly. Never had there been a cat like her. She was the prettiest cat in the world (didn't everyone say so?) and she was nice to be with (most of the time), and she ate her dinner (some of the time), and she . . . well . . . she was her cat, and she loved her. What other reason did she need?

The summer turned into fall; and when Peter went out the door each morning with books in his hand, Dorothy went with him. Calico missed her, but she never would have confessed to doing so. Besides, she soon got used to being alone. What did she need Dorothy for after all? She did not stop to think of who it was that filled her cat dish every morning with fresh food, or saw to it that she always had fresh water, or cleaned her litter box regularly.

Calico spent her days shut in the bedroom. Taffy was somewhere else. Calico wasn't sure where, but she knew that Dorothy was very careful to see to it that the two of them were never left together. It was rather unfortunate really. There were many days when Calico was bored. She could have done with a bit of sport. She tired of sleeping. She tired of watching the foolish birds fluttering about aimlessly in the back yard. She did not want to play with the ball or chew on the catnip. She wished that Dorothy was there so that she could pretend that she didn't want to be petted.

One day when Dorothy came home, she rushed, as usual, to the bedroom. Calico wanted to run to her, but she sat quite still and looked at her disdainfully. Then she deliberately turned her head back to look out the window.

Dorothy came and scooped her up. She held her closely and stroked the fine fur. It was all that Calico could do to keep the purr from escaping her throat.

"Tomorrow is Saturday and I don't have to go to school," said Dorothy in a little sing-song voice. "Mama said that we can go for a picnic. Won't that be fun?"

Calico didn't know a thing about a "picnic" but, if it meant going someplace and doing something, perhaps it would beat the boredom of the bedroom.

"It will be so much fun," continued Dorothy. "I can hardly wait. Daddy and Peter are going to do some fishing. Mama is just going to relax, and you and I can explore all we want to."

"Explore." It was a new word for Calico, but it sounded rather exciting, and she was so tired of just sitting around staring at things or being bored to death with these simple people. It seemed that Dorothy was a bit of a bore herself. All that she wanted to do lately was to sit with her books saying words over and over. She liked it if Calico sat with her, but Calico liked to be petted and stroked when she sat next to Dorothy, and sometimes Dorothy forgot what she was supposed to be doing and went right on with her words with no stroking at all. Calico would give her dirty looks then and slink off to the bedroom. Sometimes Dorothy did not even seem to notice Calico leave. That annoyed Calico even more.

Yes, thought Calico, *"picnic"—whatever it is—might be a nice change.*

She was up even before Dorothy the next morning, wondering what was taking the family so long to wake up and get going. The house was soon a buzz of activity. There seemed to be a great many things that one had to take along on a picnic. Calico thought that they would never finish packing the car.

At last Dorothy announced that they were ready to go and scooped Calico up in her arms. She ran to the car and crawled into the back seat. Peter was already there and, to Calico's horror, he held Taffy on his lap.

Calico was about to refuse to go if they insisted on taking the dog, but then she thought of another dull day spent at home alone in Dorothy's room and she reconsidered. She would go, but she would ignore the animal the whole way to wherever they were going to find the picnic.

Peter had been warned before they left home, so he held Taffy securely, the dog's back to Dorothy and the cat. Even the children were quiet as they traveled through the

city streets and out into the open country. Calico could feel the excitement in the hands that were holding her, but Dorothy managed to keep it to herself. On and on they traveled and Calico was getting bored. She tried to pull away from Dorothy's hands, but Dorothy held her firmly. If this was having a picnic, Calico didn't think much of it. Once they had left the city streets behind, there wasn't even that much to see.

Peter held Taffy up to the window and let him look out at all the farms that they passed. It seemed to amuse Taffy. Now and then he would give an excited little *woof* or a sharp *yip*. Peter tried to quiet him.

"It won't be long now, boy," Peter said. "We are almost at the stream, and then you can run all you want."

The dog seemed to understand Peter and became even more excited. Calico was a bit annoyed that Taffy, who usually looked for a chance to get at her, was now riding in the same car and ignoring her completely. For a moment she considered making a bit of trouble. The only thing that made her change her mind was that there wasn't any place to hide.

They passed through a small town and made a sharp turn down a dusty road. They hadn't gone far when they were surrounded by trees. The road continued to twist back and forth, in and out, and before long the red car pulled up beside a stream of water and came to a halt, with little billows of dust swirling all around them.

Dorothy waited for a few moments before she opened her door, but Peter was out immediately. Taffy bounded ahead of him and landed on the ground running. They raced off toward the stream, Peter yelling and Taffy barking. Calico looked after them in disgust. *What an uncivilized way to act,* she thought.

"Come, Calico," said Dorothy, picking up the cat carefully. "Let's go and explore."

Calico could hardly resist. There didn't seem to be much else to do. She didn't even ask to be let down. She had no desire to be down in the dirt. Why, it would take her hours to clean her coat if she paraded around in the stuff.

The father and mother were busy pulling out of the red car all of the things that they had spent the whole morning putting in. It didn't make much sense to Calico, but who was she to say so? She allowed herself to be carried on down to the stream as Dorothy exclaimed over the sparkling water, the bits of colorful flowers that still remained, and the small rocks that lay on the banks in abundance. It was all rather a bore.

Dorothy's one free hand was soon full. She tried stuffing things under her arm and carrying them against her body. It didn't work well, and Calico felt that she was getting the worst of the deal. Why couldn't Dorothy carry her with both hands the way a cat should be carried? Dorothy must have thought of it too. She headed back to the car. The mother was stretched out on a blanket enjoying the still-warm fall sun.

"Mother," said Dorothy, "I'm going to leave Calico in the car for awhile. I can't find stones or flowers or leaves if I have to carry her."

The mother did not even look up from her book. "All right, dear," she said.

Dorothy put Calico carefully in the car and shut the door. Then she returned and rolled both back windows down just far enough so that Calico couldn't squeeze out.

"So you can have fresh air," said Dorothy, as though the fresh air was something to treasure.

Calico jumped up into the back window and sat looking out. There was nothing to see, really. The wind was chasing a few leaves over the dead grass, and a few birds twittered foolishly as they flitted here and there. Calico had seen it all before in the back yard at home. She yawned and jumped down out of the window and curled up on Dorothy's sweater on the seat. She might as well have stayed at home. A picnic? Big deal!

When it was time to eat, Dorothy came again for Calico. She shared bits of a tuna fish sandwich with her. Calico turned up her nose at the bread but licked daintily at the tuna and butter. She drank sparingly from her water dish that had been brought along and wondered what would happen next.

Peter was too excited about the fish he had caught to be very interested in eating. All he could talk or think about was getting back to the stream. Fish were smelly, disagreeable things, and Calico couldn't think why he should think that catching them was such a triumph.

Chapter 12

Left Behind

In the afternoon, Dorothy went off to "explore" again, and as before Calico was put in the car and left all alone.

"Why don't you let her run?" asked Peter.

"She might get lost," answered Dorothy.

"Taffy runs and he don't get lost."

"Taffy's a dog. Dogs are different than cats."

"Yeah, I know. Dogs are smarter."

"Not smarter," protested Dorothy loudly. "Just different."

"Smarter," insisted Peter.

"They are not. No animal is smarter than Calico," Dorothy was yelling loudly now.

"Peter," said the mother, who had returned to her blanket and lay with her eyes closed, "why don't you go back to your fishing?"

Peter turned to go, but he couldn't resist one last barb. "Yeah," he whispered, "she's so smart she don't even know enough not to get lost."

Dorothy wanted to yell after him as he ran down the path, but she was afraid that it would anger her mother, so she let him go. She'd get even with him another time. Calico was *too* the smartest animal ever.

She went back to look for more pretty stones, and Calico curled up again and tried to sleep. She wasn't even tired. What a boring way to spend a day. *The next time that Dorothy suggests a picnic, I'll hide under the dresser,* she told herself.

At long last the family was being gathered for the trip back home. As the things—the many things—were again being pushed and poked into the car, the children were told that they could take one last look at the stream. This time Dorothy took Calico with her.

Calico was still annoyed at being so ignored all day. *Why should I be stuck in the car and neglected when even the dumb old dog got to come and go as he pleased? Besides, I'm tired, tired, tired of being carried around all the time.* Taffy was running and seeming to have a wonderful time. Calico wasn't sure that she really wanted to run in all of the dust and dead grass. Taffy's coat looked a real mess. *And I've got to ride home in the car with that!* Calico thought. No, Calico wasn't sure if she wanted to be down on the dirty ground, but it was the principle of the thing. And then there was Dorothy. Who did she think she was to come and go as she pleased, expecting Calico to always be there waiting for her? She was miffed with Dorothy.

Just as the children reached the water's edge, Dorothy spied another pretty stone and, holding her cat with only one hand, she reached down for it. It was the chance that Calico had been waiting for. Quick as a flash she was gone, leaping to the ground before Dorothy even had time to make a grab for her. She turned and headed for the trees, expecting Taffy to be hot in pursuit; but she had dashed so quickly that Taffy, who was busy chasing a stick, had not even seen her go.

Without Taffy barking at her heels, it seemed

unnecessary to climb anything; so Calico simply crawled away under a thick bush instead.

Dorothy was running through the woods calling her name frantically. Soon she was joined by Peter. He, too, was calling for her. The father came.

"Put the dog in the car, son," he said. "He will just frighten her."

Calico smiled to herself. At least she had accomplished one thing. Taffy was now forced to have *his* turn in the car. Fair was fair.

Peter went to do his father's bidding, and then all of the family spread out and searched and called for Calico. She chose to ignore them. On and on they searched and called.

"Do you think that Taffy might sniff her out?" asked the mother.

"Even if he did, it would likely just scare her," responded the father.

"But she might tree, and then we could get her," persisted the mother.

"It's worth a try. Peter, go and get Taffy, will you?"

Taffy came and this made Calico angry again. Taffy had only been in the car for a few minutes while she had been in the car for most of the day. She chose a tree nearby and climbed up onto a branch, careful to conceal herself with a clump of colorful fall leaves. *Cats are stupid, are they?* she thought. *Well, I'll have them know that I'm one cat who isn't as stupid as they think.*

Taffy did not turn out to be much of a tracker. He ran around in circles, enjoying the game that he thought they were playing. He barked and ran, and ran and barked; but it had nothing whatever to do with Calico.

"It's no use," said the father softly to the mother. "If she's running, she could be miles away from here by now."

They still continued searching and calling. Calico stayed put. She was tired of sitting in the tree. Besides she was getting hungry, but she refused to come down.

"It's getting dark," the father said to his family, but to Dorothy in particular. "We'll have to go home."

"But we can't just leave her," Dorothy cried.

"We'll have to. We'll stop in the town and post a notice with someone, leaving our phone number and name. There aren't many cats marked like Calico. Someone is sure to spot her."

"But she—" started Dorothy.

"I'm sorry, Dorothy, but it's all that we can do. We can't stay out here all night."

"But Calico will have to," sobbed Dorothy.

"Well, our staying too won't help her any. Besides she's a cat."

"But she's never stayed out before. She won't know how to keep warm or anything."

"Sure she will. Cats have instinct."

They finally all climbed in the red car; and it left the area, kicking up dust as it went. Calico waited to be sure that they wouldn't be back. She was stiff from her awkward position in the tree. Besides, she was hungry and thirsty. She backed down the tree and headed for where Dorothy had set her dish. To her surprise, the dish was not there. Calico nosed around in the gathering darkness, but she couldn't find it. There was no water dish either. What had Dorothy been thinking of? What would she eat if Dorothy didn't see to it that she had her food? Dorothy knew how delicate her stomach was. Calico thought of the place where they had shared their picnic lunch. Perhaps there were some of the tuna sandwiches left. She crossed quickly to the site and went carefully over the spot, her nose leading the way. She found no tuna. There were only two pieces of dried bread crusts and a chunk of potato chip. Well, Calico was not *that* hungry. She pushed it aside disgustedly and went to find some water. She could smell water, so it shouldn't be a problem.

The strong water smell came from the nearby stream. There was lots of water there alright, but most of it was beyond the reach of a cat's short neck. Calico stretched toward it, but she couldn't reach it. Her throat felt parched and dry. She decided to follow the stream for a ways and see if there was a place where the bank came down more gradually to the water's edge.

It seemed that she had walked an awfully long way before she found a spot. Her feet were aching, her fur dirty and entangled, and her spirits low, before she finally was able to bend her head and lick up a few drops of water. She was getting cold, too. Where was she to sleep? How she longed for the warmth of Dorothy's bed. Maybe she should have gone home after all. Then Calico straightened her shoulders. *I don't need Dorothy. I don't need the food dish or the water dish or the warm bed or—any of it. I'll show them. I'll show them all. I am quite able to take care of myself. I did find water, didn't I?*

She passed through some tangled briars to try to find herself a soft and hidden bed. The thorns caught at her coat and tore at her sides. She cried in pain and struggled to free herself. She learned quickly that one did not look for a bed in a briar bush. Calico traveled on, not even stopping to lick at her wounds.

At last she settled for a few dry leaves that had been driven by the fall wind into a little pile beneath a big fallen tree. It was not warm, nor even too soft, but it was better than nothing. She curled up tightly and tried to sleep.

There were many strange sounds in the night. Calico was glad that she had spent so much of the day sleeping, for she didn't know if they were friend or foe, so she dared not expose herself. She lay where she was, hoping that she was hidden from unfriendly eyes. She shivered, more from fear than from the cold. Would morning never come?

Morning *did* come, with a splash of color. The sun reddened the sky, and the birds of various hues began to dart back and forth in the branches. The wind increased and chased flocks of colored fall leaves dancing and playing over the ground. For a minute, the kitten in Calico came to the fore. She had the silly urge to run and chase the leaves in their wild flight, but she quickly stilled it. She was a full-grown and dignified cat. She did not do such things any more. Then she looked down at her silky coat. Well, it *had been* a silky coat. Now it was covered with dust and bits of dead grass and small twigs. It was already tangled and matted from the briar bushes. Here and there a ragged scratch had been bleeding. She didn't look very dignified or ladylike at the present.

Well, Dorothy can brush it all out, thought Calico and then checked herself. Dorothy was no longer around. She, Calico, was on her own. She had *chosen* to be on her own. Well, she would make out just fine. She didn't need any of them. She'd show them. She'd show them all.

Calico crawled from her uncomfortable bed and stretched some life back into her legs. A drink seemed to be the first order of the day. She headed back to the stream and the place where she had found water the night before. As she bent over it, she was horrified to see how dirty it was. Had she really drunk from this—this muddy puddle? It had been dark the night before and Calico had not seen just how bad the water was. Well, surely she could find something much better than that, she decided; and she set off. First, she would go back to the picnic site and see if she had overlooked anything the night before. She was very hungry. If she didn't get something in her stomach she would soon collapse.

She reached the picnic spot and looked thoroughly.

There was nothing but the broken potato chip and the two dry bread crusts, and now they were even drier than before. Calico looked carefully around her to be sure that no one was watching. There was no one. Hungrily she ate one dry crust after the other. It made her even thirstier than before. She must have water. She would try the stream again.

Calico retraced her steps down the banks of the stream, but still was unable to find any place where she could get down to the edge of the running water for a drink. At last, in desperation, she returned to the spot that she had used the night before. She closed her eyes tightly so that she wouldn't need to look at what she drank and lapped up the dirty water thirstily.

She felt a little better after having a drink. She still was very hungry, but she supposed that there must be lots of food in the forest. After all, she had seen signs of other animals living there, and they must get their food from some place. She'd just have to look for it, that was all.

All day long Calico walked and searched. The sky darkened and the wind grew chill. On she went and on she looked, poking her nose into places that she thought might possibly contain something that was good to eat. She was thirsty again and she was now a long way from the river. Her feet were sore and her back aching. She wondered why she had ever taken Dorothy's care—the dish with its clean water, the daily fresh food, the warm shared bed—for granted. She had been foolish—foolish indeed. Now she was on her own, and she didn't seem to be doing too well at it.

It was getting late and cold, and Calico still had found nothing to eat or drink. She needed rest and she needed warmth. She decided to look for a bed. There didn't seem to be a suitable place to sleep, either. She found a fallen log which provided protection from the elements to some degree and curled up in the leaves and moss at the base of it. She was still cold and she still ached all over. Her hungry tummy rumbled as it pleaded for food. Calico tried to ignore it, but it was hard to do so. She made an effort to draw the leaves in more tightly around her, but they seemed to keep scattering. At last she was able to go to sleep, even though shivers continued to shake her body.

Chapter 13

Misery

In the middle of the night, the rain came. The fallen log and its bit of overgrowth did not keep the rain from dripping on Calico's back. She hated the wet. She always had, but she hated it even more now. She had never realized before just how cold it could be. She moved slightly over and curled into a tighter ball. She still could not avoid it. *Drip. Drip. Drip.* It continued, down off the side of the big log and right onto Calico.

Calico shivered and tried to move back out of the way. It dripped then on her other side. *Drip. Drip.* She shifted again. A big drop landed on her head. Then another. Calico shook her head angrily and moved back the other way again. It was no use. No matter where she moved she could not get all of her body out of the rain.

She lay shivering. The wind had turned even colder, and the chill of it on her wet skin seemed to draw all of the warmth out of her body. She would have gotten up and left if she had had some place to go. There was no place, so Calico stayed where she was.

Morning finally came, but there was little improvement

in the weather. Calico crawled stiffly out of her wet bed and started out again. Already her feet hurt and she had not even begun to travel. She stopped for a drink in a small puddle. At least the rain had done her one favor. It had provided her with some much-needed water.

Food was still a problem. Calico had never been a hunter. She had no way of knowing that one could survive on field mice and small birds. She was still looking for a dish filled with processed cat food to miraculously appear out of nowhere.

On she went, and on she searched. At length she saw some buildings. It was a farm. Where there were buildings there must be people-persons, reasoned Calico, so she headed for the buildings with a quickened pace. *Food,* she kept thinking. *There must be food there.*

Calico arrived at the farm house with the intention of going right up to the door and asking to be let in and fed. She had never been mistreated by people-persons before, and she did not expect to be mistreated now. She saw no reason why they shouldn't be just as happy to see her as she would be to see them. After all, she was a very pretty cat, and people-persons seemed very pleased with cats.

As Calico entered the farm yard, she passed through a flock of chickens that were feeding and clucking and strutting about. Calico was quite oblivious to the chickens. She hardly even noticed them, but they noticed her all right. Squawking and fluttering and scolding her for the intrusion, they cleared her a wide path.

A woman-person appeared quickly on the porch of the house. She carried a broom in her hand, for she had been sweeping her kitchen. She looked for the cause of her frightened chickens and saw Calico just about to climb the back steps.

"Whoo!" she cried, waving her broom right in Calico's face. "Shoo! Get out of here!"

Calico stopped short. What did this woman-person mean?

"Shoo!" she cried again and waved the broom even closer. "Get away from my chickens, you hear?"

Calico took a few steps backward, looking around in bewilderment.

"Get, I say!" said the woman, and she batted Calico with the straw end of the broom.

Calico left then. She did not look very dignified as she streaked across the farm yard, dirty and still wet, her coat tangled and carrying clinging leaves, her head down and her tail tucked between her legs.

"Get away from here and stay away," called the woman after her.

Calico ran until she was exhausted before she stopped. She had meant no harm. She was only hungry. Why didn't the farm woman know that? If something had been stealing her chickens, it certainly wasn't Calico who was the thief.

When Calico finally slowed down to a trot, she was able to do more serious thinking about her situation. There was water around now. She had only to find a small mud puddle for a drink. She still needed food. She needed it badly, but Calico had no idea where to go to find it. So she just kept on traveling—traveling with no place to go.

It was late in the afternoon before Calico decided to take a rest. She still hadn't found any food, but she was just too tired to move on. She crawled in among a thick tangle of limbs and leaves and curled up for a nap. Though her body ached and her stomach complained, Calico did fall asleep. Never had she been so weary.

It was the sound of a cat that awakened her. She didn't know how long she had slept, but the sun was no longer in the sky. A cold moon hung up there now. It dived in and out of the clouds, playing—as Calico could remember she and Sister doing in the newspaper in the bottom of the big glass cage where they had lived together for such a short time. That all seemed so very long ago to Calico.

Again Calico heard a cat. It was an angry sound that was answered by another cat. Back and forth the angry cries rang. They were accusing one another of dreadful things. Calico didn't know whether to venture out to see what was going on, to tuck tail and run away as fast as she could, or to stay right where she was in the hopes that she wouldn't be discovered.

At last her curiosity drove her from cover. What in the world could they be so angry about? She crept stealthily forward and peeked through the tall grass. Inch by inch she moved, and then she found herself at the edge of a big hole. Up from the bottom of it all kinds of strange and unacceptable smells came drifting. Occasionally Calico also got a momentary whiff of something that smelled *almost* good. Her stomach churned even more.

Calico's eyes were drawn away from the big hole to some rocks about halfway down, when another wild shriek from an angry cat tore at the blackness of the night. She looked in the direction of the sound and discovered the two of them. Because of the darkness and the dirtiness of their coats, Calico could not even tell what colors they were. That they were very angry was quite evident. That they intended to do something about it was also plain. Calico had never lived in the world of cats. She had no idea what they might do.

Step by step the cats approached one another. The one on the right seemed a bit bigger than the one on the left, but he was no angrier. Never had Calico seen such rage. They shouted and screamed insults and challenges as they closed the distance between themselves. Step by step, step by step, screaming and hissing and spitting out threats. Calico could not take her eyes from them. She sat as one paralyzed, waiting for she knew not what.

Suddenly the left cat leaped directly at the right one. Calico felt herself flinch as though he had leaped at her. There was a terrible commotion. Screams and angry cries filled the air; and feet and tails and flashing claws seemed to be flying in every direction. Calico could not believe her eyes. That cats would behave in such a manner was completely foreign to her.

At last there was a break. The cats drew apart, still spitting and snarling. Calico thought that it was over, but they retreated only a few steps and started the whole procedure over again. Again Calico watched. They repeated everything that they had done before. Calico could not help but wonder what fun they could possibly be getting out of it. But they did not quit.

The left cat seemed to be only tiring, but the right cat had a tattered ear that was spilling blood down over his face and into his eye. Still they continued. They changed positions so that the right cat was now on the left and the left cat on the right. Then they went at it again, screaming and name-calling and lashing out with claws and teeth.

Calico caught another whiff of something from the depths of the big hole. Her eyes left the two scrapping cats for a moment and searched out the blackness. The moon chose that moment to come out of hiding, and Calico was surprised to see movement down below. She studied it carefully. It was another cat. And another. There were four in all. Calico could not believe her eyes. There they were just below her—feeding. Yes, *feeding*. They seemed to be completely unaware of the terrible battle that was going on just up above them.

Calico decided to move on down the steep slope and check things out. As the moved forward, one of the other cats down below also moved. A big straw-colored tom sitting nearby hissed out a warning. The smaller cat did not turn aside. With a lash of an angry tail and a quick leap forward, the big cat landed right on the smaller cat's back. There was a moment of cries of pain and anger and then the smaller cat was running for her life, up and over the many heaps and mounds in the big hole; and the big cat went grumbling back to his feeding.

Calico stood still. She had no intention of getting too near the bigger cat. She looked over at the other two cats. They continued feeding as though nothing out of the ordinary had happened.

Up above the two big toms continued their war; but nobody, not even Calico, paid any attention to them.

Most of the contents of the big hole were not edible. Even those things which might be considered chewable were not always desirable, Calico found. She worked her way over the nearby pile, choosing carefully what to put in her mouth. It was a difficult task for two reasons. One, she was terribly hungry; and, two, there really wasn't much choice. She soon decided not to be so picky. Anything that would fill her stomach and stay down would help. And so the finicky, fussy Calico found herself feeding on half-rotten discards in the area dump. She did not pretend to enjoy what she was eating but there was really no choice.

As Calico ate she moved slowly over one pile after the other. The noise of the toms had stopped. They had now crawled off alone to lick their wounds and plan their revenge. Calico had not even noticed when the last screeches had lingered in the night air. She forgot about the toms; she even forgot about the other cats, so busy was she filling her empty stomach.

Suddenly, from nowhere, a wild scream rang out; and, with it, flying through the air, came the streak of another cat. There was no time to apologize; no time to even duck. Unknowingly, Calico had ranged into the area of another of the garbage dump cats. She tried to leap away but she was not quick enough. The other cat had caught her totally by surprise. She felt the sharp sting of open claws as they tore across her face and caught her ear. Pain seared through Calico. Awful pain. And then there was the taste of salty blood as it ran down her face and dripped off her chin. Calico ran. Never had she been so frightened. The other cat did not follow, but returned to her own scavenging. Calico did not look back. She ran until she was ready to drop. She was thirsty again after all of her running—thirsty and tired and frightened and alone. She had thought that she was safe among her own kind, but obviously she was not. Where could she go? What could she do?

She stopped long enough to lap up a drink from a rain puddle and then hurried on. She could not go further. She had to rest. She drew apart into a thick tangle of dead things and tried to repair her torn face. It was difficult to care for. Calico could not reach much of the wound with her tongue. She licked at what she could and rubbed a wet paw over the rest of it. It stung to her touch. The pain stopped her from doing more. She curled up in a miserable and lonely ball and went to sleep. Why had she ever been so foolish as to leave the home where she was loved and cared for? If only she knew the way back. But Calico knew that they had traveled for many miles in the big red car. There seemed to be nothing to do but to endure the hardship that she had brought on herself.

Chapter 14

A Change of Heart

The next morning Calico climbed wearily from her bed. Her sleep of the night had not seemed to refresh her. Indeed, she had had very little. She had spent most of the night traveling and eating at the dump. She had not eaten enough though, and her sides pressed together for lack of something to hold them apart.

She started out on her search for food and water. The rain puddles were already drying up. The smaller puddles had completely disappeared. Calico traveled for some time before she found one that could still offer her a muddy drink. She lapped up the water, not even bothering to shut her eyes.

Her search for food was without reward. All day she wandered and sniffed her way across the countryside but she found nothing. At night she found herself on the edge of the big hole again. There just didn't seem to be any other way to survive.

Calico checked carefully for other cats before she made her descent. There were three of them. Calico chose to enter the excavation at the point farthest away from any of the cats. She picked her way carefully over the heaps of rubble, checking frequently to see if she might be approaching any of the other inhabitants. When she found herself getting near one of them she quickly changed her course.

There were fights; each time that one of the feeding cats felt that another was infringing on his or her rights there would be a row about it. There was always a winner and a loser, and some cat always looked a little worse for the tangle. Calico saw scars and torn ears and half-closed eyes. The cats of the dump seemed to live by the law of the claw.

By the time morning arrived, Calico was almost full. Some of the night's picking had been a little rancid and didn't set on her stomach too well, but she did feel almost comfortable. The other cats must have felt the same way; for they began, one by one, to leave the area. Calico couldn't help but notice that they all seemed to head in the same direction. With a good bit of fear, but even more curiosity, she decided to follow them.

She had not traveled far when she came to an old deserted building. By sound, rather than by sight, she discovered that the cats were somewhere under it. She could hear bickering and complaining. She waited until things seemed quiet and then ducked down and entered. For a while she could see nothing, and then her eyes began to pick out shapes and outlines. She saw a number of cats. No two of them were close to one another. It seemed to be the unspoken law that no cat should remain in the close proximity of another.

Calico picked a far vacant corner and moved toward it. A big black female raised her head and stared at her with cold, angry eyes.

"So you think you are moving in?" she said. "Just like that! First the dump and now the house. You just move in at will, do you? No questions asked. No permission requested, just—"

"Oh, hush up," growled an even bigger tom. "I'm sick to death of your continual complaining."

"An' I'm sick of the both of you," came a third voice from a rangy male in the corner.

"So who asked you?" spit out the tom in the direction of the other cat.

"I don't wait to be asked," he answered, and there was challenge in his voice.

"Maybe you should," the tom answered him, not even flinching. He turned again to the female, ignoring the male in the corner. "Besides," he said, "isn't that how you came to be with us, Your Highness? You just walked in like you owned the place, if I remember right."

The female snarled and left to go out and lie in the sunshine. The tom looked pleased with himself for putting her in her proper place and curled up for some sleep.

Calico tried to sleep too, but she got very little. Always, always, some of the cats were scrapping. Mostly it was just angry, cutting words that flew back and forth; but sometimes they resorted to blows. Calico abhorred it and pulled even more deeply into the corner.

That night they all crawled forth, without spoken agreement, and traveled to the dump again. They did not travel together in any kind of companionship; but rather they all went alone, choosing their own time to leave. Calico was hungry again so she did not wait too long.

The wind was blowing again. The temperature had dropped. The night air was bitterly cold. It had been much warmer in the sunshine. Calico found herself wondering why the cats chose to visit the dump by night instead of by day. But somehow it seemed fitting. Who would want to be seen in the dump in the broad daylight?

Calico fed. Tonight, the garbage did not seem so repulsive to her. Perhaps it was because she was hungry, or maybe she was just getting used to it.

In her wandering she came upon a choice piece of beef-steak fat and bone. It was not even very rancid, and Calico reclined on the heap of rubble and began to devour it with relish. Another of the cats had smelled it too and moved over with the intention of stealing. He grabbed the one end of the bone and began to tear it away, snarling and threatening as he did so.

"Give it to me," he demanded.

"I had it first," insisted Calico.

"Give it to me," he said in a louder more persistent voice.

"No," shouted Calico, refusing to let go.

"We'll see," snarled the young tom and took a swat at Calico with outstretched claws. Calico felt the sting of the claws as they scratched across her shoulder. For a moment she considered leaving the bone and running, and then a terrible anger took hold of her. She dropped the bone and sprang directly at the other cat, catching him completely by surprise. Over and over they rolled, screaming and clawing and tearing at one another. When they finally broke, it was the small tom that ran off to lick his wounds. Calico, still seething with anger, went back to claim her precious bone. It was not there. While the fight had been going on, one of the other cats had stolen it.

Calico looked about her, still angry. She could not see the cat with the stolen steak-bone, but she did see a small tabby nearby munching on a piece of dry bread. Calico sprang at her for no good reason, catching the poor soul completely off guard. She dropped her crust of bread and fled from Calico's presence. Calico should have felt good about it, she told herself, but she didn't. She felt miserable. *I've become just like them,* she said to herself. *Here I am fighting over their garbage. Brawling—like a common alley cat.*

The thought did not please Calico. She was not proud of what she had become. Well, she might never be able to find her way home again, but surely she didn't need to stoop to this. She left the garbage dump without even a backward glance or a goodbye. Behind her she could hear the angry voices of fighting cats. Calico wanted no part of it. She had been above all that once. She might not be able to climb back to her former status, but at least she would not sink so low. She would live off the fields—would starve if need be—but she would starve with dignity.

She began to travel—to put as much distance as possible between herself and the quarreling cats and the garbage dump.

There was no food to be had that first day. Calico did find a bit of water but not enough to really quench her thirst. On she went, always heading in the direction that she felt was home.

At night she crawled under a culvert and tried to sleep. It was cold. The night air went right through her thin, matted coat. Calico shivered where she lay and closed her eyes tightly against the bitter wind that somehow found its way even into the small culvert.

The next morning Calico set out again. Again she traveled without food. There seemed to be nothing that Calico could find to eat. Her sides were gaunt and sunken. Her shiny coat was messed with dirt and debris, her scratched face gave her a lopsided look, and her torn ear flopped crazily as she ran. There was little resemblance to Dorothy's well-groomed and well-fed cat, but Calico was unaware of her appearance as she continued on her way. She was thinking only of getting back home—back to Dorothy—back to those who cared for her. She would show them all how she had changed. She would no longer be proud and picky. She would not strut or complain. She would no longer be bored and stuffy. She would even make friends with Taffy. Calico realized that she might never be fussed over again because she was the prettiest cat in the world, but there was a chance—just a chance—that she might be one of the nicest.

On she ran, placing one weary and bleeding foot ahead of the other, willing herself to keep moving—keep moving. She was so tired that she could have dropped, but she pressed on. On, and on, and on.

Calico looked up as she traveled and saw the outline of a town. It brought hope to her heart and her weary body. They had traveled through a small town on the day that she had come with the family on the picnic. It seemed like such a very long, long time ago. Calico tried to get her tired legs to move just a little bit faster, but they would not respond.

The air was very cold. Big, fluffy flakes of snow were falling slowly. Dorothy would be pleased with the snow-fall. She loved the snow. For Calico it was an added burden. It made her travel even more difficult. The snow made the grass and ground slippery and soggy. It was even harder for Calico to lift her tired feet.

On and on she went until she came to the town. She looked this way and that trying to find a landmark that she remembered. Up ahead she spotted something that looked vaguely familiar—a sign on a building. Calico thought that she had seen it before. On past the building she went, always looking for more clues as to the direction she would take. One by one, she picked things out and traveled forward.

At last she came to an intersection busy with cars. For a few moments she was lost. Which way had they come? Calico saw nothing to give her any clues; and then, way down the street, she spotted a house with a strange roof. She had remembered seeing it before. She headed for it. Cars seemed to be buzzing all around her. Calico coaxed her stiff legs and sore feet into moving faster and made a dash for it.

She was across. By some miracle, it seemed, she had

made it. She headed on down past the house and on beyond, looking for another sign, another clue. She was almost through the small town now. She felt that she knew the way to go to reach Dorothy. It was across the next intersection and on down that street that led to the highway. Then she must travel the many, many, many miles down the highway to the city where Dorothy lived.

Calico made a dash for it. Her stiff legs did not work well. A black object passed over her head. Suddenly she seemed to be surrounded by screeching tires, and then everything went black—very black.

Chapter 15

Mrs. Brown

The little lady stepping out briskly beneath the protection of the rainbow umbrella was Mrs. Matilda Brown. The day was a nasty one. Folks would be complaining. Nobody was ready for snow to arrive so early in the fall. Nobody enjoyed the heavy clouds when they wished instead to see sunshine. Everybody would be out of sorts and grumpy. Mrs. Brown had her job cut out for her today. She must try to bring some cheer into the lives of those people who had so little to be cheerful about. *I suppose that those with rheumatism will be even more uncomfortable today. Those with dark-day blues will be even bluer. Yes, I've certainly got my work cut out for me. There will be many people needing cheer today.*

Mrs. Matilda Brown was just the lady to bring it. She had learned, though not through ease or pleasure, that it paid to have a cheerful outlook. Being angry or upset with one's circumstance never did seem to improve the circumstance. Handling the situation with cheerfulness might not bring too much relief to the actual circumstance either; but it did help one to be able to bear it a little better. Mrs.

Brown had vowed that she, with God's help, would face each one of life's situations with as much cheerfulness as He could give her.

And so she stepped along smartly, looking forward to her volunteer work at the local convalescent home. She didn't need to go. She probably wouldn't even be expected on such a day; but she wished to go, for she felt that there were people there whom she might be able to inspire and comfort.

Mrs. Brown looked both ways to be sure that no traffic was coming and then stepped out into the intersection. She was about to pass on when a tangled bit of something caught her attention. She moved toward it and found it to be a cat.

"Why, a kitty," she exclaimed. "It must have been struck by a car."

Mrs. Brown bent to touch the piece of fur just as a shudder went through the small body.

"It's alive," said Mrs. Brown in astonishment and looked about her for something in which to wrap the unfortunate cat. There was nothing. Mrs. Brown laid aside her umbrella and removed her coat. Then she slipped out of her sweater and replaced her coat again. She bent over the senseless creature and carefully—oh, so carefully—moved it onto the sweater. Then, holding it firmly and gently, she gathered up her umbrella, and sheltering the poor little thing, she headed again for home.

As soon as she had deposited the little bundle in one of her soft chairs, she went to the phone.

"Millie," she said to the person who answered, "do you think that you can get along without me today?"

There was a moment of silence while the other person talked.

"No, it's not the weather. I was coming anyway, but I found this poor miserable little kitty that has been struck

by a car. It's still alive and I hope that I can do something for it."

There was more talking on the other end of the line.

"Thank you, Millie," said Mrs. Brown. "I knew that you would understand. I must go now."

Mrs. Brown at once set to work over the cat. She had not been called the best nurse in the county for nothing. Her hands moved gently over each of Calico's bones. She found no broken ones.

"The car passed right over you. You are lucky. You must have been under it and been struck on the head. I just hope it wasn't too bad a blow, that's all."

Her fingers continued to feel out each part of the cat's body.

"My, but you are thin," she said. "You mustn't have had a decent meal for days.

"You really need a good vet," she continued, "but we have none in town and I don't have a car. The only bus to the city has already gone for today, so I guess we'll just have to do what we can." And Mrs. Brown went to work with all of her nursing skills.

It was not until the third day that Calico finally lifted her head for the first time. She had been strangely aware through some kind of haze that hands were touching her, caressing her, coaxing her back to life, as they gently stroked liquid down her parched and burning throat. She did not know whose hands they were, but she learned to be deeply grateful to them. There had been a soft voice, too.

She saw a face now, a kind face, bending over her, through the haze of her unfocusing eyes. The hands continued to stroke and caress. The voice spoke gently. Yes, the hands and the voice must belong to the face. Calico tried to move, but her body would not cooperate.

"It's good to see you awake at last," the kind voice said. "I had about given up on you."

Calico laid her head back down on the soft bed again and shut her eyes. The whole room was whirling around and around. She wanted to stop it if she could. But the room did not hold still until Calico fell back to sleep.

The next time that she awoke, her head felt much better. She still was not able to move her aching body, but she was able to swallow on her own. The little lady was pleased.

"That's a good sign," she said. "You're making some progress. Before we know it, you will be as good as new."

But it was several days until Calico was as good as new. In fact, her progress was very slow; but it was steady. Always the kind lady was there with her, encouraging her and caressing her. The day finally came when Calico struggled to unsteady feet. She stood swaying slightly.

"Don't you try too much, too quickly," the kind nurse scolded. "I've known people like you. They were never willing to give nature the time to heal them properly."

Calico laid back down on the soft bed again and rested. The next time that she got to her feet, she felt a little steadier. And the next time was even better. And finally she was able to stand alone with no difficulty.

She noticed that her sides were still thin, and she felt very hungry now. She cleaned up every meal that she was given. Remembering her past experience she never refused what she was fed. It was always so much better than the food that she had scavenged in the dump. She also remembered the many days with no food at all. She was tremendously grateful to the little woman and took every opportunity to tell her so.

"You need a name," announced Mrs. Brown one day. "I'll call you 'Ginger.' "

As Ginger regained her strength the little lady turned her

attention to her untidy coat. "My, what a mess you got yourself in," she exclaimed, as she brushed out dirt and clipped out burrs. "Why, I don't know if I'll ever get you clean again."

Ginger also took an interest in her appearance again; and, when the kind Mrs. Brown was off doing her volunteer work at the convalescent home, she would spend hours cleaning and shining her coat. There was nothing that she could do about the scars or the torn ear. They were grim reminders of an unwise choice in the past.

The wintry days passed by. Ginger grew more and more attached to Mrs. Brown. She was there at the door to meet her each evening when she came in. Mrs. Brown was equally delighted to see Ginger. They sat together before the open fire in the evenings as Mrs. Brown read to herself and scratched Ginger on her one good ear. Ginger purred loudly and rubbed her face against the loving hand.

"What a warm and affectionate thing you are," said Mrs. Brown. "It's almost as though you are trying to say, 'I love you.' "

Time moved on. Christmas came and went. In her love for Mrs. Brown and her happiness in being with her, Ginger seldom ever thought of Dorothy. When she did, it was with sorrow that she hadn't been kinder and more appreciative when Dorothy had been so good to her.

One day when Mrs. Brown returned from her day of volunteer work, Ginger noticed that she was troubled by something. It wasn't very often that Mrs. Brown allowed trouble to show on her face.

Ginger, in her concern, was especially loving. Mrs. Brown held her close.

"I'm so lucky to have you," she whispered. "You have a way of making me forget my sorrows. If only poor Mrs. McDonald at the home had a cat like you. She's new there, you know; and she doesn't feel that she has a friend in the

136

world. I tried to get close to her but she shut me out. Poor soul." And tears trickled down the face of Mrs. Brown. Ginger reached up and licked one of them away. Mrs. Brown began to laugh and pulled her close.

"You funny cat," she said, but there was laughter in her voice and joy in her heart. "You should be the one visiting the home—not me." And then a strange look came into Mrs. Brown's eyes. She placed Ginger carefully on the floor and went to the phone.

"Millie," she said, "I have just had a wonderful idea. What if I bring Ginger in with me tomorrow and let her cheer up some of the patients? There's that dear Mrs. McDonald. She doesn't want any of us to do anything for her, and she is so lonely. Then there is little Tommy Blake. He hasn't spoken a word since his horrible accident . . . and Mr. Crowder—"

Mrs. Brown was interrupted by the voice on the other end of the phone. It seemed to go on and on, but finally it was Mrs. Brown's turn to talk again.

"Then it's settled. Oh, I'm so excited. I can't wait to try it. They are using it in many homes and hospitals, you know. They call it 'Animal Therapy.' Often very ill people will respond to animals when they won't respond to other people."

There was more talking from the other voice. Mrs. Brown looked more excited every minute.

"I know they are careful to use an animal that is loving toward people, and I know that it needs to be very gentle; and Ginger is. She has the sweetest disposition of any cat that I have ever had—and I've had a number of cats over the years. She's just perfect for it; I know she is."

Again there was more talk.

"All right," said Mrs. Brown excitedly. "I will bring her tomorrow. We'll try her first with Mrs. McDonald; and, if that works, we will see about letting her visit little Tommy.

Thank you, Millie. I'll see you tomorrow.''

Mrs. Brown returned to Ginger with her eyes glistening.

"Oh, Ginger," she said, picking the cat up and holding her close. "I am so happy. From now on, you will be a volunteer cat. You'll bring so much joy to those poor suffering people at the home. Just think of it, Ginger. A real chance to serve—to serve and to love.''

Ginger thought of it. It seemed like some kind of a miracle.

Chapter 16

The Home

The next day was Ginger's first day as a volunteer at the home. She was excited about it, but she was nervous too. She didn't have any idea what to expect. It helped tremendously that Mrs. Brown was also going. Mrs. Brown knew all about the home. She also knew all about Ginger. She would not allow anything unpleasant to happen to her. Ginger had complete faith in Mrs. Brown

They entered the wide doors together, Ginger held firmly in Mrs. Brown's arms. A strange, somehow familiar, smell met Ginger's nostrils. For a moment she wanted to run, and then she remembered Mrs. Brown and all of her kindness. If there was any way that she could show her love to this woman, she was willing to try. She steeled herself against the smell and the clean polished look and tried to relax.

There were women-people at the desk and they fussed over Ginger, stroking her now shiny coat and remarking about her pretty coloring. It no longer went to Ginger's head. She remembered what she had been when Mrs. Brown had found her.

"Where is Mrs. McDonald this morning?" asked Mrs. Brown.

"She's still in her room. She refused to wake up, even for her breakfast."

"Then I guess that Ginger and I will just pay a little visit to her room."

They found Mrs. McDonald with her back to the door. She didn't answer the greeting of Mrs. Brown, nor did she turn to look at them.

Mrs. Brown went around to the other side of the bed. Ginger saw the eyes of Mrs. McDonald quickly shut against the intruders.

"Mrs. McDonald, I brought you a special visitor today," said Mrs. Brown.

There was no response.

"She wants to visit with you—but she doesn't talk much; so you might have to do all of the talking."

Still no response.

Mrs. Brown reached for the thin frail hand and lifted the fingers. There was no resistance but no response either.

Mrs. Brown placed the fingers against the warm fur of Ginger. Still no reaction from Mrs. McDonald.

This isn't going to work, thought Ginger and she felt sorry for Mrs. Brown after she had tried so hard.

"Now, Ginger," said Mrs. Brown, placing Ginger gently on Mrs. McDonald's bed, "I want you to stay right here and visit with Mrs. McDonald for a while. I will be back later to get you."

Ginger snuggled up against the form in the bed. Mrs. Brown took one of Mrs. McDonald's thin, lifeless hands and placed it on Ginger's back. Then she smiled encouragingly at Ginger and left the room.

The day was long for Ginger. She spent it all with Mrs. McDonald. She pressed her nose against the hand and purred. There was no response. She rubbed her cheek

against the arm. There was no recognition. She meowed talkatively. The eyes did not open. Lunch time came. A nurse entered the room and spoke cheerily to Mrs. McDonald. She did not answer. They rolled her gently on her back and offered her soft food on a spoon. She swallowed very little of it. A straw was placed to her lips and she drank a few swallows. The nurse left again. Ginger tried even harder; it was so important to Mrs. Brown. Ginger really felt no love for the mute old woman who laid so lifelessly on the white sheets, but she did love Mrs. Brown; and, to Mrs. Brown, Mrs. McDonald was very important, so Ginger stayed with her—a warm, living something under the touch of her hand.

Mrs. Brown came in. She stroked Ginger fondly.

"That's a good girl," she said. "Just stay with her; let her know that you are here. That's all that you need to do."

She left again, and Ginger pressed her nose into the frail hand. She purred more loudly and pressed her warm body against the arm of the woman. In the late afternoon, just before Mrs. Brown came to take Ginger home, an amazing thing happened. There was just a touch, just a small movement of two outstretched fingers. Mrs. McDonald had made a small effort to stroke the cat.

They repeated the long vigil the next day, and again the next. Ginger still wasn't sure that it was working. Perhaps she had only imagined the slight movement of the hand. On the fourth day, just after the lunch hour, Ginger witnessed another miracle.

Mrs. McDonald opened her eyes and looked directly at her; then she reached out with a wavering hand and ran her fingers over Ginger's warm fur.

Another day went by. Mrs. McDonald had her eyes open much of that day, and she watched Ginger—watched her every move. Ginger was sure not to lie still for too long. For some reason that she couldn't understand, she felt that

142

it was important to make Mrs. McDonald's eyes keep searching for her. Still she never left the woman's side. She made sure that her body was touching the body of the elderly woman in some way all the long, long day.

There was no way that Ginger was able to communicate to Mrs. Brown what had been going on in the sick room. Each day when Mrs. Brown came to collect Ginger for their walk home, she saw only the still form of the old woman. She was waiting for some outward sign that the lady was responding to Ginger in some way.

She received the sign the next morning, for when she arrived in the room with Ginger in her arms, the elderly woman had her eyes open. She was awake and aware. She moved slightly and, ever so feebly, lifted her hands toward Ginger to welcome her to her bed. Mrs. Brown placed Ginger in the old woman's hands with tears streaming down her face.

Ginger spent many more days with the elderly Mrs. McDonald. Her improvement was slow. At times there were even setbacks, but eventually she was able to sit up in bed and even to feed herself with her spoon. Ginger was her love and her joy, and she watched eagerly every morning for the cat to arrive.

"Ginger can only stay with you for a little while this morning," Mrs. Brown informed her one day. "There is someone else that she must visit. I'll bring her back in to say goodbye before we go home."

Disappointment showed in the eyes of Mrs. McDonald.

"A very sick little boy needs her badly," went on Mrs. Brown, and Mrs. McDonald reluctantly nodded her head. Mrs. Brown left Ginger and went to visit other patients. Mrs. McDonald reached for the cat. Her hands were much stronger now as they stroked Ginger's soft coat. She even spoke a lot. Ginger could never untangle the words and the stories. They seemed all mixed up and confused—the past all intertwined with the present—but Ginger purred and meowed and pretended that it all made perfect sense; and that was all of the assurance that the old woman needed.

When Mrs. Brown came to get Ginger, she carried her to a small room where a sad-eyed little boy lay propped up with pillows. Ginger had never seen such a pathetic looking child. His body looked whole, but there was a vacant look on his face and his skin was very pale. When Mrs. Brown presented Ginger, he reached for her eagerly with both hands and held her so tightly against his chest that Ginger could hardly breathe.

"If you are very nice to the kitty, she will visit you for awhile, Tommy," said Mrs. Brown. "You don't need to hold her so tight. She won't run away."

Tommy did not relax his hold.

"Here, like this," went on Mrs. Brown, and she re-arranged the small boy's hands. It felt much better to Ginger.

"She likes to be stroked softly—like this. And she will sing for you. Listen."

Obediently Ginger began to purr. Tommy's eyes widened.

"Do you like the song?" asked Mrs. Brown, but Tommy made no reply.

"You lay and listen to her, and she will sing for you—just for you," said Mrs. Brown. And giving Ginger one last affectionate pat, she left the room.

Ginger continued to sing. She looked directly into Tommy's eyes and meowed. She rubbed her nose against Tommy's cheek and licked at his face. Tommy seemed to enjoy it all, but he said nothing.

Mrs. Brown came for Ginger and, as promised, took her in to say goodbye to Mrs. McDonald before they went home. The old lady smiled. It was her first smile since she had come to the home. Mrs. Brown left the two of them alone for a few minutes. Mrs. McDonald stroked Ginger

with stronger, but rather clumsy, hands. She talked her senseless words, and Ginger sang her a song.

"She'll be back in the morning," Mrs. Brown smiled, when she came back to pick up the cat.

The next morning, after spending a short time with Mrs. McDonald, Ginger was taken to see Tommy again. They spent the day together—in silence, except for Ginger's purring and occasional *meow*. At the end of the day they visited Mrs. McDonald again.

The next day went much the same. There was more light in Tommy's eyes as he reached out his hands for Ginger; but there was still silence, though Tommy did sit up in bed to play with the cat.

Another day passed by and another. When Mrs. Brown came to collect Ginger for her daily trip back to Mrs. McDonald, Tommy shocked them both. "I want to keep her," he said, holding fast to Ginger. The words were clear and unmistakable, but they were the first words that he had spoken for many weeks.

Mrs. Brown tried to control her desire to shout for joy. She waited for a moment until she was sure that she could speak without weeping and said very softly, "I'm sorry, Tommy, but there is a very ill lady in one of the other rooms. I promised her that Ginger would go in to see her for a few minutes before we go home."

Tommy's eyes filled with tears.

"I will be sure to bring her back to see you tomorrow. How's that?"

The boy said nothing more, only let the tears fall. It was the first time that Tommy had cried in many weeks as well. Many of those who cared for him had said over and over, "The poor little boy. If only he would cry." But Tommy had not cried. Not until now.

Mrs. Brown sat down on the bed beside him and pushed

back the unruly hair. Then she leaned over and pulled the small child into her arms and held him closely against her. Tommy continued to cry, great sobs that shook his whole body and left him hiccupping. Mrs. Brown held him and loved him, allowing him to weep for as long as he cared.

At last he pushed back from her and lay back down.

"I'll leave Ginger with you for a while longer," Mrs. Brown whispered. "We really aren't in any big hurry to get home today."

She left the room quietly, and Tommy scooped the cat back into his arms and held her against him. There were no more tears now. He pressed his face against the fur of the soft animal and talked. He said all sorts of things. Things that he never would have confided to his doctor or one of his nurses. He shared how he dreamed bad dreams at night; he told how he didn't have a home to go to anymore. He told how alone and frightened he was now that his family was gone. He didn't want to go to live with his aunt and uncle, he said; he didn't even know them. Then he cried some more. Ginger licked at the salty tears and purred in Tommy's ear.

By the time Mrs. Brown came back to gather up Ginger, all traces of Tommy's tears were gone. He was all talked out as well. He lay back on his pillow, a very small boy with a very big hurt, but the haunted look was gone from his eyes.

"Remember, I promise to bring Ginger back tomorrow."

"Why can't she stay?" asked Tommy.

"She can't stay, because she is very tired. All good nurses are tired by the end of the day, and that is sort of what Ginger is. An animal-nurse. She comes in to help sick people get better. By the end of the day, she is weary and needs her rest—just like I do."

"Do they pay her?" asked Tommy in surprise.

"Oh, no. Ginger doesn't get paid. She comes because she

loves you and wants to help you get better.'' Mrs. Brown
saw a chance to press a point. ''Will you do that for her,
Tommy? Will you get better real fast? It would make
Ginger so happy.''

Tommy looked doubtful, but he reached out a hand to
Ginger and tickled her fur with his fingers.

''If I get better,'' he said slowly, ''they'll send me to my
uncle's.''

''I've been thinking about that,'' said Mrs. Brown. ''I
was wondering if they could send you over to my house
when you are well enough. Just for a while—until you have
a chance to get to know your uncle a little better. I've met
them, you know, both your uncle and your aunt. They are
wonderful people. Really! They would be here with you
now if they could. They were here for many days, when
you were still too ill to remember. They had to go home to
their family. Do you remember your cousins?''

Tommy thought hard. ''Only a little bit,'' he said.
''They live too far away.''

''Well, you have a cousin, David, about your age. And a
cousin, Stephanie, older than you, and a smaller cousin,
Shelley. They can hardly wait for you to get well enough to
join them; especially David.''

''I don't know,'' said Tommy glumly; and Ginger was
afraid that he was going to cry again.

''Well,'' said Mrs. Brown cheerily, ''we won't worry
about that now. First we want you well enough to come
and spend some time with us. Can you do that?''

Tommy nodded solemnly.

''Now, tell Ginger goodbye.''

Tommy reached out a hand to stroke Ginger, but he said
nothing.

''We'll be in in the morning,'' again promised Mrs.
Brown and she left with the tired Ginger in her arms.

Chapter 17

The Surprise

The days went by. They visited the home almost every day. On Sundays Ginger was allowed to lay and sleep while Mrs. Brown was at church. In the afternoon, they often went for a brief visit to the home, if Mrs. Brown thought that there was someone there whom it was urgent for them to see.

Mrs. McDonald never did get so that she could get out of bed again. She did gain some strength and was much more attentive. She even got so that she could entertain herself with TV on occasion. And she talked to her nurses, though her talking often did not make much sense, save only to her. Still, the nurses were pleased with her improvement.

Tommy continued to make progress. He was anxious now to be well enough to leave the home. Daily he talked with Ginger and played with her. The day came when he was strong enough to leave his bed. He took Ginger with him to the sun room and the game room after that and the two of them did many things together.

As promised, Mrs. Brown was making arrangements for

Tommy to come to her house for a few weeks, as soon as he was able to leave the hospital.

Ginger was shared with other patients as well. Old Mr. Crowder never did seem to know that Ginger was sharing his bed. After many days of no response, Ginger was not taken to his room any more. Mrs. Valetti was able to grin and pat Ginger whenever she visited her. She seemed to enjoy the closeness of the cat. She spoke to Ginger in words that Ginger could not understand. There was no one else in the home who could understand poor old Mrs. Valetti either. Mr. Crane did not like Ginger. His gnarled old hands would reach out and pinch and poke her. Ginger tried to stay calm and not cry out when Mr. Crane mistreated her. She dreaded her visits to Mr. Crane and endured them only for Mrs. Brown's sake. When it was discovered just how hurtful Mr. Crane was to the cat, Mrs. Brown stopped Ginger's visits to the room.

So there were days of triumph and days of disappointment. Many of the patients seemed to be cheered and encouraged by Ginger's visits to their beds.

Easter brought good news. The doctor had declared Tommy well enough to be moved to the Brown household. Mrs. Brown informed the home that she would take some days off to give all of her time and attention to her small guest. She did just that. Of course she had Ginger to willingly help her.

The days with Tommy went very quickly. He improved with each one of them. His aunt and uncle phoned frequently, and Tommy was able to speak to them as well as to his cousins. He and David became good phone-buddies. They shared many interests and began to be excited about getting together. It was arranged for David to come for a few days. He had a weekend plus two days free from school.

At first the two boys were a bit shy and seemed as

though they might talk with one another much better with a phone in their hands; but when Mrs. Brown called them to the kitchen for chocolate chip cookies and milk, they seemed to feel more comfortable. From then on they had great fun together.

Tommy was well enough to go out with David to fly kites. He even seemed to lose some of his need for Ginger —though he still took her to bed with him each night.

The four days passed very quickly. It was soon time for David to go home.

"I wish you were coming with me," he said to Tommy.

Tommy looked a bit uncertain.

"Well," he said slowly, "I will when— I will—after—" He cleared his throat and straightened his shoulders. "I will," he said.

Mrs. Brown wisely said nothing.

David left on the afternoon bus and Tommy went home to watch TV. The cartoons were not as funny anymore, with no one to share the laughter with. It was no fun to fly kites alone, either. And one could not play checkers all by oneself.

After two days Tommy came to Mrs. Brown. "I've been thinking," he said slowly. "Would you be awfully lonely if I went to David's now?"

Mrs. Brown pulled him into her arms. "I will miss you very much," she said sincerely. "Both Ginger and I will miss you. But you're right. You belong at David's house. You will be happiest there."

And so Tommy packed his things, and his uncle came and got him. He was excited about going, though he did hate to leave Ginger and Mrs. Brown.

"You can come back and see us—anytime," said Mrs. Brown, and Tommy agreed. He phoned often the first while, but his phone calls became fewer and fewer. He was back in school and he was in Little League; he had his own

bike; he helped David deliver newspapers; and he was
happy—he had a family.

After Tommy left, Mrs. Brown and Ginger began their
daily visits to the home again. Mrs. McDonald was no
longer in her bed. Another lady had the room now.
Another lady that needed a friend. Ginger was often taken
to see her. There were other patients too, and Ginger tried
to be as agreeable and loving as she could. She grew quite
fond of some of them, and then there were a few others
that she wished to avoid.

The days went quickly by and another summer came and
went. The whole staff at the home regarded Ginger as a
very important member of their team.

One day Mrs. Brown had stopped for coffee with some
of the girls, and Ginger purred contentedly on her lap.
Peggy Sawyer reached out and stroked Ginger's fur.

"She really is a pretty cat," she said affectionately.
"I've never seen one with prettier markings."

"It's a shame about the ear," said Wendy Clemski.

"I wonder just what happened to it."

"Do you suppose that it could be repaired?" suddenly
asked Ida Lynn.

Mrs. Brown put down her tea cup and looked down at
Ginger, fingering the torn ear gently.

"Oh, I'm sure that it could. It would just need to be—"

"Then why don't we?" cut in Wendy excitedly.

"Well, a good vet costs a great deal of money. I'm
afraid that I just don't have it, and it doesn't seem to cause
her any pain."

"I know, but she'd look so much prettier with it fixed."

"Yes, I suppose she would."

"Then why don't we?" asked Wendy again.

"Well, I really don't—" began Mrs. Brown, but Ida
stopped her.

"No, not you. All of us. We are indebted to her. She

works for *all* of us. We'll all chip in."

"Great idea," said Peggy. We'll start a 'Ginger Fund.'"

"But—" began Mrs. Brown. "I really don't think—"

"No 'buts,'" Wendy said. "I'll get it started."

And so a fund was started to provide surgery for Ginger's torn ear. Even the doctors threw in some money. The word got around and soon there were patients wanting to be a part. Mrs. Brown thought that the Ginger Fund brought more interest and healing to some of the patients than anything that had been done for them thus far.

The fund grew, and it was soon time to make the date with the veterinarian surgeon in the city. Peggy was the one who drove Mrs. Brown and Ginger in to the doctor's office.

Ginger was a bit nervous. Somehow she knew that she was the cause of all of the commotion. She was much relieved that Mrs. Brown was still with her when they all climbed in the car and headed out of town. As they traveled, she noticed things along the highway that were strangely familiar. She wondered when she could possibly have seen them. And then she remembered the long-ago picnic.

As they drove through the busy city streets, she became more and more uneasy. If it had not been for the calm hands of Mrs. Brown she would have been terrified. Somehow they kept her steady.

At last the car came to a stop and Mrs. Brown lifted Ginger and followed Peggy into the doctor's waiting room. Ginger looked around her, her eyes wide with wonder. *I've been here before,* she thought. *I know that I have been here before.* And then she remembered. This was the place where she and her sister and brothers had been brought as kittens. This was the place where she had been returned for a shot. This was a place that she did not like nor trust. Her whole body tensed.

"It's all right," said Mrs. Brown gently. "It's all right,

Ginger. I am right here with you.''

Ginger relaxed again.

A woman-person in a white coat came forward.

"So this is the cat for the ear job," she said in a pleasant voice.

"She's a bit frightened," said Mrs. Brown. "Do you mind if I just hold her for a few minutes?"

"Why don't you just bring her on back? Come this way."

The lady in the white coat led the way, and Ginger found herself in the room with the high, white table. Two people were there—the man in the white coat and the lady in the white coat.

The man took Ginger and looked at the ear carefully. His hands also passed over the rest of Ginger's body, searching out every bone.

"She seems in good shape except for that ear. How did she do it?"

"I don't know," said Mrs. Brown. "I found her in the street. She had been hit by a car. But the ear wasn't torn then. It was already partly healed."

"Strange," said the man, studying the ear more closely while the woman held Ginger firmly. "Looks almost like it was done by another cat."

"Something about her—" began the woman. "Something about her seems so familiar."

"I was thinking that, too," said the man.

"I know," said the woman. "The kitten. The kitten that the little Warren girl took. I'm sure it's her. There just couldn't be any two cats with these same markings. She is one of the prettiest cats that I have seen."

"I think you're right," said the doctor.

"I remember now," said the woman. "The little Warren girl lost that kitten. About a year ago now. Her mother brought her back in for another one."

Mrs. Brown sat very quietly. She had not had reason to

suppose that the adventures of this day might take Ginger from her.

"Are you *quite* sure?" she finally asked softly.

The woman suddenly remembered the quiet lady who sat in the room. She hardly knew how to answer her. It was apparent that Mrs. Brown loved the cat deeply.

"Well, I don't suppose there is any chance that Dorothy would want her cat back now," she hastened to say, "not after all of this time."

"They brought back that second kitten," said the doctor, without thinking. "Dorothy said that it just wasn't like her Calico."

"Calico," said Mrs. Brown. "The name suits her."

Mrs. Brown stood to her feet. "Do you have her number?" she asked in a strained voice.

"They have it at the desk," the nurse said kindly. "But are you sure—?"

"We must know," Mrs. Brown said resolutely. "If Ginger is a little girl's cat, then she should be returned."

A call was put in to an excited Dorothy. Her cat may have been found. She was now in surgery, Dorothy was informed, to repair a torn ear. If she still wanted the cat, she could meet Mrs. Brown at the doctor's office the next day and see if it really was her.

Mrs. Brown did not sleep much that night. Her thoughts were continually on Ginger—or Calico—whatever the case. She would be so lonely without her. And what about all of the patients at the home? Many of them had grown to love their little "animal nurse," as they jokingly called her. But fair was fair. If she belonged to Dorothy, then she most certainly should be returned.

Wendy again drove Mrs. Brown in to the Animal Hospital the next day. The doctor had reported that the cat had come through the surgery just fine and he had every reason to hope that the ear would heal with very little

damage showing. Since Mrs. Brown was a nurse, the doctor was willing to let the cat go home again. She would rest better at home than in the hospital, he felt.

When they reached the hospital, Mrs. Brown hurried back to see Ginger; and Wendy sat down in the waiting room with a magazine.

A little girl took the chair next to Wendy. Excitement showed in her eyes. She could hardly sit still, and she kept checking the clock on the wall.

"She should be here now. She said two o'clock," she whispered to her mother.

"She'll be here," promised the mother.

"I wonder how Calico looks," went on the little girl. "Will she still know me, Mother?"

"I think so. Cats have very good memories."

Wendy smiled at the little girl. "You're here to pick up a cat?" she asked.

"Yes," said Dorothy, anxious to talk to someone. "She had surgery."

"Is that so?" said Wendy. "I'm here to pick up a cat from surgery, too."

"Mine is a very *special* cat," said Dorothy. "She's the prettiest cat in the world. But I haven't seen her for ever so long."

"Mine is a very special cat, too," said Wendy and then she began to laugh. "Well," she said, leaning closer to Dorothy, "she isn't even *my* cat. But I love her anyway. She belongs to Mrs. Brown, and Mrs. Brown is a lady who does volunteer work at the convalescent home where I work. There are a lot of very sick people there, and Mrs. Brown comes in almost every day to help them to get better, and she brings Ginger with her.

"Now, you might not believe this, but Ginger is the *best nurse* that we've got." And Wendy went on to tell the wide-eyed Dorothy all about Ginger, the Animal-Nurse-

Cat, and how she had helped many people get well.

The time passed quickly, and soon Mrs. Brown was walking toward them with the cat in her arms. But Wendy and Dorothy were too involved to notice. Mrs. Brown's steps slowed as she saw the young girl who was talking with Wendy; then she lifted her chin determinedly and moved forward. "Are you Dorothy?" she asked in a kind voice.

Dorothy swung around to look at her. Mrs. Brown looked down at the cat in her arms. "Is this—? Is this—?" she tried to ask.

"Calico!" cried Dorothy and buried her face in Calico's fur. Calico remembered Dorothy. She remembered all of the times that Dorothy had held her and groomed her. She remembered the fresh water and the good food. She remembered the shared bed and the gentle stroking. She lifted her face and kissed Dorothy's cheek in deep gratitude. But she did not leave the arms of Mrs. Brown. Dorothy's tears were falling on the soft fur.

Wendy had risen to her feet. "Calico?" she echoed. "Calico?"

"This is Calico," said Mrs. Brown. "Dorothy's lost cat."

"But—but—" began Wendy. "This is our Ginger."

Dorothy turned to look at her, unbelief showing on her face. "This—is—is Ginger?"

"Yes, we brought her here to—"

"This is the 'animal nurse'?"

"That's right."

Dorothy turned back to the lady before her.

"Are you Mrs. Brown?" she asked.

Mrs. Brown nodded her head silently, placing the cat in the little girl's arms.

"And you take Calico to help people get better?"

"That's right. Ginger—Calico—and I have been visiting the home together for many months now."

Dorothy stepped back toward Mrs. Brown. "It wouldn't

be fair," she said. "It wouldn't be fair for me to take her away from them—or from you, after—" But Dorothy could not go on, for she was weeping.

Mrs. Brown reached out and drew both the little girl and the cat named Calico into her arms.

"You can take her back—back to the people," sobbed Dorothy.

"Are you quite sure?" Mrs. Brown asked at last.

Dorothy nodded her head and reached up to wipe away her tears.

"Let's sit down and talk for a minute," said Mrs. Brown and she led Dorothy to a private corner of the room.

"It's true that I love the cat very much," Mrs. Brown said, "But I know that you love her, too. I was glad to help her, to nurse her until she was better again. But Dorothy, she is your cat. If you want to take her home with you, then you may."

"But the people—" said Dorothy. "The sick people at the home."

"Yes, they would miss her very much."

"Then she should be with them."

"You are a very unselfish little girl. I will tell all of the people at the home about you. Maybe someday you can come and visit with them too."

"Oh, could I?"

"Certainly. And you can stay at my house. Summer vacation will soon be here; I'll ask your mother."

Dorothy's face lit up. She passed the cat to Mrs. Brown, and this time Mrs. Brown accepted her.

"And we will call her Calico," Mrs. Brown said. *"Calico* suits her *much* better than Ginger."